# Any who catches my eye can have me

Jim O'Donoghue

First published in 2021
by LateVixenBooks

Printed in England by Clays Ltd, Elcograf S.p.A.

ISBN: 978-1-7398080-0-6

**Enquiries to the author should be directed to:**
jimodonoghue@hotmail.com

In memory of Martin Fry. This is instead of a bench or a tree, old man. We still think about you and talk about you and miss you.

# The Turkish Casino

It was late when he got off the train at Lewisham, close to chucking-out time. He glanced around, briefly wondered where he was but then wandered as he always did. He walked down by the Quaggy River, a shallow trickle between concrete banks, to the high street, a slumberous void at that time of night, strewn with Burger King wrappers and pages of the West End Final. He must have been here before – over the years, he'd been everywhere – but he must have left almost at once, since he had no memory of the only real landmark, a villagey little clock tower. No one was around, not even a dog out walking itself. An hour or so after sunset and the vacant lanes still ran with dark heat, swirls of scorching air spinning down shadowy passages between streetlamps and bins, although it was still only April.

But tomorrow was May Day, of course. As he dawdled by the window of a convenience store, not sure what to do in such a dreary spot at such an hour, a frail old lady in a shellsuit appeared out of nowhere. On another night her terrified glance might have struck him as bizarre, the way she flinched at the sight of him and scuttled on – but tonight her fear seemed natural. Her alarm took him back to the moment earlier in the evening when he was standing before the tinted glass doors at Centre Point, grooming himself, and it happened: a sort of tearing in the air as if a small but significant number of the city's population had been sucked into the cloudless sky, a solitary scream. Like everyone else, he'd turned towards the source of the sound less than half a mile away and seen nothing, only noted the silence that followed. Then he'd walked quickly into Covent Garden, to loiter in a daze for hours while the sky grew dark, until in the end the piazza was overwhelmed by people coming from Soho, and he'd taken a train at random to get away from the crowds.

It was his habit to take random trains – often he'd travel to the end of the line and come back – and it was only by chance that he got down at Lewisham, after the drunk who sat opposite him suddenly barfed at his feet. Otherwise he would have gone on to God knows where, if not to the terminus then the end of the zones. He might have opened a window and smoked a cigarette, if there were no guards around, or written something in his notebook. But to escape the rank smell and the depressing guy with his puke-encrusted shoes, he'd left at the next stop.

Now he tossed the end of his fag into the gutter and crossed over to Ratners, to run his eye over all those dinky pieces of gold, or gold-plating. Some men had enough cash to throw away on trinkets for their sweethearts, which seemed an extraordinary indulgence to him, when he could just about afford his rent and a train ticket, a secondhand paperback and a refill for his hipflask. He felt a stab of sadness at the thought that he'd never buy a girl a ring. He might have retraced his steps and left Lewisham for good – really for good, because he refused to return to any place where he'd been unhappy, however temporarily – if he hadn't glimpsed a door ajar beside the jewellers' barred windows. On its blistered paint, someone with a shaky hand had scrawled the word GAZINO. Emboldened by some strangeness in the night, he pushed at it and climbed a flight of stairs.

In a room at the top, he was greeted by a profusion of reds – plastic chairs in the kind of toffee-apple red he remembered from fairs in his childhood, flocked wallpaper with a ruby stain. A cerise carpet clung to the soles of his shoes as he crossed it as casually as he could, aiming for the bar. From the bar he turned to look back at the scene that dominated the middle space: beneath a long lamp, at a baize table in flaming cochineal, a ring of Turks

6

with serious faces placing their scagged chips, intent on their game and nothing else. The grotty doorway and dim staircase had hinted at nothing so exotic as this gambling den. How easy it was to break into another world, he thought. Only a minute before, this red room would have been beyond his imagination.

It was a members' club, and at the bar of scratchy crimson formica a rotund man he took to be the owner explained that to buy a drink he'd have to fill out an application form. He nodded; his presence was neither welcome nor unwelcome, just another aspect of a life that everyone in the room seemed to take for granted. The big guy called to someone in the cubbyhole that served as a kitchen before going off to his counting house in back, and in another minute a waitress emerged with a form printed wonkily on a limp piece of A4.

He'd put it down in a puddle of beer, taken out his pen and written his name before he realised that the form was written entirely in Turkish, with no translation. He looked quizzically at his waitress, but she only glared back at him with a frown that might have been drawn on her face by a child with a scarlet felt tip. She continued the theme to her hair, which was crudely hennaed, giving her an older woman's look out of keeping with her lingering puppy fat. She was in her mid-twenties, he reckoned, a few years his junior, one of those surly migrant girls who could be found all over the capital, working 24/7 on illegal contracts and evidently hating every second.

He gestured at the soggy form. 'I don't know what it says – and it's not as if I even want to gamble.'

'Then what are you doing here?' She moved along the bar, wielding a mucky J-cloth, frowning steadily.

He grinned at her frown, a trick that occasionally had an effect. 'The door was open, so I came in.'

'Are you actually from the police?' She glanced towards the back room, where her boss sat at his desk with an ear pressed to a portable radio, puffing on a thin cigar. For the moment, she was in charge. Anomie flitted across her cheekbones; whatever her origins, she was a proper Londoner, a little Miss Urban Paranoia.

He shook his head. 'As a kid I thought it would be great to be a cop – you know, pointing out short cuts, telling people the time. Perhaps I was naive.'

'Naive,' she repeated thoughtfully, looking at him for the first time with some attention. 'I like that word. It's the same in my language.'

'Really? What language is that?'

She let go of her rag and held his eye, tugging at her bra-strap between the buttons of her white blouse. A badge pinned above her right breast read MONIKA. The gamblers had paused in their game to watch them talk; the stocky croupier in a burgundy blazer a size too small also stood watching, his hand on the wheel.

'I come from a small country,' she said. 'You won't have heard of it, no one does. No one ever goes there – everyone leaves.'

'Sounds like my kind of place. Maybe I'll go there myself, if things get too much for me around here.'

At that she smiled at him, the curl of her bright red lips like a vamp's in a vampire movie, and he saw she was not just another sullen waitress, angry about her tips. She had a face full of hectic allure, girlish and unfinished, a look that would age but never ripen.

'You don't have to fill in a form if you only want a beer, *Dean*,' she said, reading his name to him from the form.

He drank his beer at the bar and watched the game, watched the wheel slow with its dizzying solemnity, the ball clattering to a halt on all those magic numbers. At the game's end, the players took a break and sat smoking cheroots around the baize, scuffed and faded from a thousand hands of Billabong and Oxford Stud. The men looked on in quiet admiration as the waitress cleared tables, followed her with their eyes, and now and then she treated them to a flicker of a smile – but only a tame version, not her scary vampire grin. But after a second her face fell again into its expression of discontent, in which there was something oddly crepuscular. It was hard to imagine her out in sunlight; she was a Slav, he divined, from some far-flung end of Mitteleuropa, a land along the Danube where generators often failed and people went to bed by candlelight.

As he drained the bottle she was passing, and on an impulse he asked what time she closed up. He knew she must hear the same question a dozen times a week; after all, London was full of men of all ages, from all walks of life, who spent their weekends going to bars and cracking on to the waitresses, then laughing bitterly at their rejection. It was true that he'd only done it once or twice himself over the years, but that was because he only liked sure things – asking the question of women who were almost bound to say yes, who'd already in some way acquiesced. So he stood there waiting to be rebuffed, but she raised one eyebrow and said, 'Do you mean the casino or do you mean me?'

'Oh,' he said, 'I meant you.' Cloth in hand, she looked him up and down, as if inspecting him to see whether he was for real, until he added lamely, 'I'm not such a fan of roulette, to be honest – it makes my head spin. And in any case I'm down to my last fiver.'

She shrugged, as if the matter was settled, and held his eye, unsmiling. 'You can come for me at three.'

'Seriously?' He hadn't expected such instant success, hadn't really expected any success at all – he'd only been gambling on a whim. 'Where can I go till then?'

She hesitated, disappeared into the back room, and half a minute went by before she returned with something in her hand.

'Hey,' she said, leaning in and slipping a set of keys into his jacket pocket in one motion, unseen by the men at the table. In the same movement she took his pen and scribbled her address on the wilted application form, along with a sketchy map. 'You will need to take a couple of buses at this time of night,' she murmured, tapping her temple. 'It is complicated.'

'That's alright, I'm good with buses.'

She moved in close again and stayed there for a beat or two, and he picked up the scent of her exhaustion; she must have been on her feet for hours. 'When you get there,' she told him under her breath, 'make sure you go to the right bedroom. You will see a big mess on the floor, a vibrator on the bedside table and some stuff to smoke. Roll one, if you like.'

# Monika

When he went out again into the night its aspect was altered, as if a troubling vacancy had been filled, a feeling lifted, as if its violence had thrown this treasure into his lap. He caught the first bus and climbed to the upper deck. While it swept him towards his goal, he saw through the trembling outline of his reflection the wastes of suburban south London, disordered hinterlands full of cement fortresses and a thousand unlit rooms. Around him sat mumbling strangers, each absorbed in their own reflections and bathed in the same heat rushing through windows as open as they would go. They muttered and squirmed in their seats as if lost in nightmares of bloodshed, in all the weird energies unleashed into the dieseled air by tonight's main event.

Their agitation carried him back in his memory through a succession of crowds – to the last one in town before he jumped on the train for Lewisham, the small throng that hung about on the station concourse at Charing Cross, nibbling their kiosk nibbles, already forgetting the nearness of the final moment as they eyed the departure boards. Before that he'd seen from the flagstones in Covent Garden, where he sat and sipped from his flask, the flood of refugees from Old Compton Street, all stunned and frantic and wild with adrenaline – and before that he was one of many at the top of Charing Cross Road in the second when it happened, among the many heads all turned in one direction towards the still nameless incident, all those mouths open in angry wonder.

He would have reached into his pocket for his hipflask to wash away these images, but he wanted to stay fresh for his waitress. As it was, by the time he got to her flat and let himself in he was worn out by the sensation of flight and the unstoppable memories of the scenes he'd run away from, and he lay down on her bed in his boxers. It was a relief to find himself in a place so alien and full of distractions. On her bedside table he discovered, as she'd said he would, a well-stocked stash box with a silver cross on the lid. Beside it was a lamp with an orange junkshop shade, a strawberry alarm clock and a pink vibrator with a dainty prong, this last the only item not frilled with dust. Alongside these grimy objects he found a paperback with half its cover torn away for roach material, *The Celest— Proph—*. He tore off another strip, rolled a joint and lay back to watch himself smoke in a ceiling mirror that some voluptuary must have stuck up there in a more innocent decade; absorbing the smoke, he felt as if by total accident he'd found a sanctuary, a safe house so obscure that nothing and no one would ever look for him there. He turned out the light and stared for a while into the polluted shadow – the neon was strong down in the street – until, in a flash, he lost consciousness.

It was hard to pick her out from his dream when she woke him before dawn, straddling him with her thighs. She put him inside her before he knew where he was, and he experienced her for a split second as some totally wild thing, not even an animal but an atmosphere in some hidden place. She must have turned on the lamp; its orange shade cast a gaudy pall as she moved above him, forcing him to open his eyes just to check that the room wasn't actually on fire. He closed them again at once, but the dark behind his eyelids blazed with a submarine glimmer, as if he was swimming below the surface of an ocean covered in burning oil and couldn't rise to take a breath.

This went on for some time, forever it seemed, until she reached her peak and sang out and then hovered at the end of his flesh until he looked up at her again, sure it was the end. He watched her shake in her aftershocks, her features rearranged by lust and all but unrecognisable. In fact, he had no idea who she was. When she leaned in and touched her forehead to his chin, he lifted his hands, preparing to release her – but it was not the end. She started over, as if forgetting what had come already, and for an age he was so nipped in his neck by her teeth, raked along his spine by her nails and pinned to the bed by her sex that his life was just this fuck.

As daybreak found its way through her torn curtain into her bleak little room, she let go on him one last time and fell forward limply to rest her head on his chest. Through her window, open just a crack, a new but staler world tumbled in – thuds and clanks of loading and unloading, cars revving down Leigham Court Road, birdsong and bootheels of early commuters. The electrical pulse of a house alarm half a block away throbbed like hers, slowing gradually against his side until he felt it return to normal. Trapped in the ceiling mirror in that grainy twilight just before sunrise, he saw the dip of her waist and jut of her hips in all their cartoon glory, like the curves of Betty Boop. The mirror's damaged silver captured them in monochrome on her divan, his greyish pallor and her milky thing.

When finally she unpeeled herself from him and sat up, he took her hand and pressed it to his lips.

'I think you've broken my mouth,' he said, 'but in a good way.'

She laughed down at him, her thighs still straddling him for a minute, her eyes two green lakes of satisfaction. Then she got out of bed and went to an armchair in the corner and stooped to dig around in a pile of bottoms and tops, while he leaned on an elbow to count from across the room the dot, dot, dot of her vertebrae. She stood in her own kind of wasteland: her threadbare rug was scattered with chewed-up fashion magazines; there was a dirty foot spa with an inch of standing water, a cracked CD case missing its CD, a plastic water bottle she must have used for a bong. By the wall facing the window, a chest of drawers spilled lycra leggings, ankle socks, headbands and bundled underwear – savage thongs and pretty knickers, a lifetime's supply. She stood up straight again and over her hennaed head pulled on a black t-shirt with the words MILLENNIUM BUG printed in silver lettering across the chest. She turned to find him watching her and grinned her vampire grin.

'Well,' she said, 'that was me.'

She went out to pee, and he was left alone with his sudden knowledge of what he wanted, so precise for a moment and so clear. He was unsure what to do with this sudden clarity, whether to find the handcuffs that must be somewhere hereabouts and cuff himself to her bedpost or just search her sheets for a keepsake, a curl of cunt hair or flake of skin. If he couldn't stay here in this room for the rest of his life – and he couldn't, of course he knew he couldn't – he could at least take a souvenir. But no, it wouldn't do, he wanted more than a souvenir, wanted this moment to stretch out into his future interminably, to last forever. Perhaps there was a way for him to spend his life in this bed. If she came back into the room right then and stuck a blade between his ribs, it would make total sense, would be a suitable ending.

But rather than a knife, she returned with two white plastic cups, which she put down on her bedside table and filled with vodka from a quart bottle. It was a cheap English vodka, sobering rather than anything else, but the ceremony with which she served it made it taste like some vital juice. They sat and drank in silence while dawn made its progress in streaks down the soiled walls of her boxy space up on the second floor, where they floated free above the streets as if suspended from skyhooks.

'There was another bomb last night,' she said at last.

'I know,' he said, 'I was there – it could have killed me.'

She looked at him steadily from under her eyebrows, plucked into a pair of stern arcs. 'Then *this* would not have happened.'

'No, we would never have met.'

She looked down into the cup without sipping from it, as if allowing herself a moment to take in the twists of fate that had brought them together.

'It was a surprise to see you. I thought you might not be here when I got home.'

'But I had your key,' he objected, surprised.

She shrugged, drained her cup and crushed it and dropped it on the floor beside the bed. 'Maybe you decide not to come,' she said, meeting his eye. 'Maybe you get scared.' She lay down then and began to fold herself up in the off-white sheet like an origami swan until only her head, an arm and a foot were showing.

'Your English is nearly perfect,' he told her, reaching across to put his own empty cup on the table. It was true – she spoke with a kind of exacting grace, clipped and almost colloquial. 'Did you learn it here?'

'Of course,' she said, covering her eyes with an arm as if suddenly losing interest in the conversation, 'where else?'

She lay like that for a few minutes with her arm across her eyes, then all at once flung it away from herself, tearing the sheet from her body in one involuntary motion. It was much brighter now in her room; daylight drew rings around her, painted all her gaps, but it felt wrong to sit watching her and he covered her up. He lay down beside her to watch her sleep, which she did soundlessly and without moving at all, stuck to her sticky coverlet; but after a while he began to feel restless, and he got up and went over to the window. The dawn chorus was over – down in the street another morning was underway, apparently a banal repetition of all the other mornings but actually just itself, unique and brilliant. He couldn't stay forever in this room, in this moment, although it was tempting to try, and he looked around for his things and glanced at her face once more before leaving.

# Somers Town

To his sleepless mind the streets seemed psychedelic, even the static early morning traffic with hints of gridlock at every junction and the Egyptian barrow boys who sorted their veg on wooden crates. The hill tipped him down into Brixton, and he felt like running through the glittering sunlight that broke between highrises and bounced from roofs of cars, turning his walk into a mad dash along a covered arcade, through a scattered radiance that fell between arches – and for a minute his life was just a flicker.

In momentary bewilderment, although it swung from his shoulder, he believed he'd left his satchel behind. He had to check – and then he checked the hip pocket of his brown suede jacket for his hipflask and the inside pocket for his pens. Everything was still there; everything about his body ached, but then the life of his body felt imaginary, as if he swung between two worlds in which there was a real waitress and another who was unreal, a real Dean and one he'd invented. Fingering the lid of a gel pen for reassurance as he walked, he told himself that she was there at his back, swanlike and stuck to her sheets, while he wandered down Brixton Hill through pools of light.

In his ramblings he'd walked up and down Brixton Hill many times, but this morning the slope was fresh with new shadows and filled with a knowledge that hadn't been there a day before, a black lesion that was not like death but like dying, like being taken away from this tactile and tasty universe at the precise moment when you knew you meant nothing at all. The morning shone in slivers and spurs, in bright denial of such emptiness but holding on to pieces of the night, unable to forget last night's annihilation. He couldn't run from it, either. However fast he moved there would remain the threat of invisibility, of one day coming to a place with no source of natural light and being unable to leave.

His practice was to stay constantly in motion, to walk it or train it or bus it from one side of town to another, between the necessary and the contingent, taking in what he saw and taking note. At times he'd stall and stand for an hour or more in a doorway on the Edgware Road, Warwick Avenue or Baker Street, watching people pass, bewildered by his own restlessness, unable to think of a next move. But it was important sometimes to stop and look around; it was only by stopping that he'd stumbled across her, in that weird stretch of time last night when the lights seemed to go – and in that obscurity they were matched, as if the bomb had thrown them together.

These dizzy thoughts kept him company all the way to Brixton station, where he barely noticed the gurning madwoman camped at the entrance, the foul air down on the platform or slow arrival of bodies at the start of their northward trip. Exhausted, he slipped in and out of consciousness on the tube and in a spasm of forgetfulness staggered out into sunshine at King's Cross – by mistake, meaning to change onto the Northern Line. But he liked this walk, often took it by choice. It was only when he set off up Chalton Street into Somers Town that he emerged from his reverie. He saw in the blossom trees with their already half-baked blossom, naked magnolias whose petals were long since dispersed and swept up, yellow jasmine whose scent was still intense and that quiet Somers Town sultriness, shimmering and rising from all surfaces, the start of a new season. He saw it begin right in front of his eyes, in a silent unfurling. The dreams left on the other side of the river suddenly lacked all substance, seemed trapped in their locale, even as his body held on to the memory of how she felt inside and the tip of his tongue still knew her flavour. Her reality fell away, as if what was true in the borough of Lambeth stopped being true as soon as he entered Camden. Simple facts came home: that he lived in a dangerous place, but dangerous only now and then, that it was Saturday, May Day, and tonight there was a party.

Somers Town, an accidental haven between Euston's toings and froings and Camden's frenzied thrashings, held him in its spell for the ten minutes or so that it took him to cross it. Bursts of rhythm and melody came from windows open onto balconies and fire escapes, prayers to Jesus and Mohammed and chants to the Buddha, songs of the Lo Fidelity Allstars. A child spilled out onto the pavement on his bike as if ejected suddenly by the massed estates, swivelled and set off for the playground on Ossulston Street with his sister on her scooter in mad pursuit, while their mother trailed after them, drawing her palm across broken flowers on the verges of neutral, civic lawns. In this small state of serenity, he allowed himself to consider the fact that he'd been invited to a gathering of the clan, a rare enough event these days. He had half a mind not to go. Who really did he want to see – who would really want to see him? But he felt the need to celebrate this sudden riot of aromas and colours.

All winter he'd been on a retreat within city limits, sipping gimlets in a cocktail bar on Inverness

Street, rereading his favourite books, at last orders rolling down rainy routes home and talking to himself like an old friend, sheltered from harsher realities by walls of grey water. Facing up to reality was for other people, for those with money in the bank, a spouse and a safety net. He had none of those things, but it had never been his intention to acquire them. Instead he wandered the city in search of nothing in particular, eyeing up the gigantic caryatids around St Pancras Church, peering through bent railings on the Old Kent Road, drawing patterns with his Docs across London's A to Z.

Since leaving university a decade ago, he'd been through several periods of monkish seclusion, to emerge again whenever his solitude began to bother him. This morning he felt inspired – he was still alive, by sheer luck, spent the night inside a woman, magnolias were in bloom – and he felt the urge to share his inspiration. He came to the top of Somers Town, where Oakley Square opened out on the Working Men's College, a mere ten minutes' walk from home – but fatigue flooded his system and those ten minutes seemed like eternity to this working man, every moment weirdly elongated, each step a giant leap. Shadows and light overcame him, as if his mind was on the blink; he felt the waitress above him again and felt *her* inside *him*, so vividly that he clung to the brickwork before going on blindly, feeling his way.

In that weird little eternity he saw, even if straightaway he tried to forget it, how far she embodied the one-off he'd always craved: that this Dean and this Monika should meet was not some cosmic hiccup or a match made by a dating agency but a coincidence so meaningless that it meant everything. He knew she'd never get it, never know her own significance – they'd already passed each other by, even before they'd really begun. He saw it all distinctly, in the instant before he slammed his mental doors shut, a strange future in which neither understood their connection, it remained a mystery to them both.

When he came to his door he came to his senses. He must have been sleepwalking, delivered by his feet to the corner with Camden Road. Now finally he could rest – but before he lay down he'd write in his diary, a ringbound A4 notebook stolen from one of the offices he'd temped in before Christmas, on its cover inscribed with a stolen marker pen, *1999*. There was a diary for every year since he left college, stacked under his bed in his rented flat and only to be read, as he told himself sometimes with a smile, by whoever came for his things when he died. Ink was his life blood; he sat back to watch it dry, admiring his own calligraphy. This morning he'd sit at his desk and record in detail the night before, from explosion through train ride to his waitress in her dark little flat – and how before he left he printed in capitals on the flyleaf of her one stray paperback, *SEE YOU ON SUNDAY?* Then he'd give the episode a name – **The Wounded Admiral** perhaps, or **White Plastic Cups**. Or perhaps he'd just call it **Monika**.

## Stick of Tea

It was on a May Day five years before that Laura had married Alberto. Earlier in the afternoon they'd celebrated their anniversary at their home in Clapham with a bottle of champagne and a captious attempt at lovemaking. Now Laura went from room to room of the party in Shepherds Bush, averting her long face and avoiding conversation with those friends from school and university who'd been her wedding guests.

Laura had recently turned 31 and, lo and behold, everywhere she turned, everyone was 31 – but she remembered them best when they were 19 and full of tricks. They were her friends of course, this was her milieu, but she had to pretend a little these days to get along with them as they gave vent to their fin-de-siècle grouching, carping on interest rates and house prices. She listened impatiently while they waffled on with extraordinary complacency about the foibles of their partners in business and love and highlights of their incomes and outgoings. If they ran out of things to say about the real world, they resorted to idle commentary on some aspect of the cultural scene mainstream enough to catch their attention but niche enough for cred, a two-hander at the Almeida or something shocking from the Young British Artists. There was nothing personal about any of it, nothing interactive, not even in the nervous chatter of the one or two professional neurotics who gabbled with forced gaiety about their reliance on Prozac.

On the first-floor landing of their host's beautiful terraced house, Laura bumped into Carrie. Still as skinny and button-nosed as she was at 21, Carrie was a sad example of the scene's slow decay. Once agreeably bizarre, she now came across like a skittish ice maiden, her mannerisms more mannered with each passing year.

'Laura! Darling! Let's dance!'

'I'd rather not – it reminds me of my wedding day. *You* remind me of my wedding day. *He*,' she said, pointing downstairs to the dancefloor in the living room, 'reminds me of my wedding day.'

Alberto was jiving around to *Tainted Love*, his diminutive figure wrapped in combat gear bought especially for the occasion, as if every party was an excuse for fancy dress. In his khaki shirt and army surplus boots, he looked like an officer cutting loose on furlough. It was an attempt at disguise, of course; no matter what he put on or how he flung himself about to yesterday's tunes, he was the same dull soul whose tedious inner workings she'd discovered only after their honeymoon. Once she'd admired his ability to assimilate, but now it frankly irritated her, this way he had of fitting in with other people's worlds. Someone had made a mixtape of songs from an era before the age of irony: Soft Cell were followed by Katrina & the Waves yelling, 'I'm walking on sunshine!' Alberto leapt in the air and almost punched the lampshade.

'Dear Alberto,' murmured Carrie, 'he tries so hard.'

'Do you think I'd hate him so much if he wasn't my husband?'

'Oh Loz, I know you think the world of him really. I'm looking for something like that myself –

you know, someone I can worship in private and laugh about in public.' Carrie sipped daintily at her dirty Martini while Laura slugged at her glass of red wine. 'Really, you're a marvel, Laura,' Carrie said after a pause, with that mannered insincerity that had seemed so funny when they were young. 'A woman shouldn't be able to drink and smoke the way you do and still keep her complexion.'

'Oh, Carrie.'

'And your dress, oh dear, your dress.'

'Oh dear, my dress.'

Laura glanced down at the purple taffeta thing that flared to her knees; when she looked up again, Carrie, whose singleton status was like a beacon to a certain type of unattached male, was chatting away with a man in a deerstalker and corduroy trousers, an ideal candidate for public derision. Laura drifted downstairs, not in the mood for either dancing or talking, and steered a course around her husband, who bopped like someone demob happy in his moleskin trousers, his boots clattering the floor. Oppressed by the immaculate olive and ivory of her surroundings, she headed for the garden through a swarm of knackered lawyers, out-of-shape accountants and frustrated hacks. They formed their own tribe, self-selected. Alongside the happy band who'd scaled the battlements straight out of college and won a slice of the city for themselves were those who'd fallen from the ladder at the first hint of boiling oil. Tonight they mingled in bitter camaraderie, overlooking as best they could their difference in status, although the vanquished couldn't simply drain their glasses but had to earn their right to every swallow with some clever remark. Others wandered like nomads through the fine west London abode, throwing Beaujolais across carpets, burning holes in curtains and smearing walls with vol-au-vents in the knowledge that their hosts could afford a professional cleaner.

Laura walked down the long, narrow garden, turning her back on the lighted terrace. No one who looked from the kitchen door would see her out there; in her purple taffeta, she'd blend into the shrubbery. Hidden in silhouette against masses of lilacs and rhododendron, she lit a cigarette and listened to the night. A black tomcat jumped onto the fence beside her with a clatter that would have made an anxious person flinch; but Laura only scowled at the beast through the gloaming until it jumped behind bushes and was gone.

She stood and smoked for some minutes, thinking back to that fateful afternoon in Manhattan when she'd bumped into Alberto in the Strand bookshop. He was looking for reproductions of Piranesi, she was looking for Pirandello – two characters in search of a book. He was completing his masters on the economic forces in Italian renaissance art; she'd gone to New York in search of a building to adore, but she was distracted from her quest by the profusion of beautiful cocktails and even more beautiful men. Alberto was not beautiful to look at, but he thought about things and spoke with an old-school elegance. After ten minutes of conversation they became lovers, making out then and there between the stacks – another ten minutes passed, or so it seemed, and they were shacked up together in Williamsburg.

Seven years ago in New York City, poor Alberto hadn't been too hairy, too Italian or too small – he was just Alberto. She'd loved to listen to him talk about Palladio and Pasolini and Marco Polo while fellating him on their skimpy bed in their tiny apartment. When a year had passed and they were still *in love* – that weightless intangible that somehow takes up two words – he'd given up his Green Card for her and come to England. They looked in each other's eyes and saw the fear, they took the leap and timed it wrong, and something that had for a while been effortless became tawdry and strained.

Laura sighed and threw her Silk Cut into the lilacs. All at once a man – she could tell by his scent he was male – came out of nowhere to stand beside her in the dark, twitching and muttering stray little curses under his breath. He must be loaded, she knew, by the way he kept up his nonsensical soliloquy, fidgeting as if covered in ants. Just as she wondered whether it was safe to let him know she was there, he took a sideways step and bumped into her.

'Oh,' he said – but he sounded unsurprised. He must have picked up on her fragrance and known, unconsciously, that a woman stood beside him in the darkness.

'It's a hot night.'

She saw nothing of his face, only his shape filled out by shadow. 'Hot hot hot,' he agreed, holding something out to her. 'A guy just gave me a stick of tea. Do you want some?'

'Stick of tea?' Laura laughed, peering at the dense black line that was all she could see of him. 'What is this, 1957?'

'Reefer, doobie, rainy day woman, whatever you want to call it.'

'Thank you,' she said simply, and took the joint from him. When the man held up a lighter to relight it, she had an inkling of his eyes, coals with no back or front, a receding hairline and a hint of suede. Then the lighter went out, and she inhaled and saw nothing but the glowing end of the joint. It was made with pure grass and a smidgen of tobacco; she remained silent for a time, aware of a great inner rush. 'You were talking to yourself,' she said finally, when it had blown itself out.

'I know.' He took the spliff from her fingers, relit it in one easy movement and gave it an audible toke. From the lighted windows of the tall house, guests threw paper cups, cans and unwanted food, as if they were crossing the night sky in a hot air balloon and shedding ballast.

'It's a talking-to-yourself kind of party, though, isn't it?' As he handed back the spliff, their hands touched. Air's *Sexy Boy* blared from an upper storey at an impossible volume, while sprays of lilac sent a purple haze through the overheated air.

'Shall we sit down?' he suggested, promptly sitting at her feet in the rhododendron's greenish gloom. Laura sat down too, glad of the camouflage. She was super-stoned, but in the darkness it didn't matter so much if her eyes were crossed or her tongue was lolling. She felt a warm flood of sensation as a hand sought her out, starting at her calf and travelling up beyond her knee to her inner thigh. She fell back on the dry turf; a crackle in the undergrowth brought her back to her senses, and she snatched his hand from her suspenders.

'No one can see us.' His voice came from up close. She drew back a little and felt about for her cigarettes.

'I can't fuck you tonight,' she said, 'whoever you are. It's my wedding anniversary.' The man sat up straight and laughed heartily at this, and something in his laugh made her want to renounce her renunciation; there was a hiatus, in which she began to miss his wandering hand. 'I didn't necessarily mean for you to stop altogether.'

But the stranger held out the joint again, his contours clearer now that her eyes had adjusted. The inflections of his voice seemed to pencil in his features. 'I've met you before, you know.'

'Possibly you have. How long have you been friends with these people?' She gestured vaguely towards the house.

'Oh, most of my life,' he said, as if he was a hundred years old. 'Once we were all very close, but not anymore.'

'So we may well have bumped into each other before at one of these things.' She sucked hard and filled her lungs with hilarious smoke. The effort of this polite conversation brought her to the brink of hysterical laughter.

'Oh, I don't think so. I just mean that I've met a lot of women like you,' he said, 'married women who want to ripple their pool.'

'Ripple my pool?'

'Do I use too many metaphors? Shall I get literal?'

'No, not at all,' she giggled, feeling ridiculously elated, beautifully mad. 'You're quite right. I do have a pool, and I do throw stones into it from time to time.'

She tried to hand back the spliff, but he waved it away. 'Nah, keep it,' he said, 'it's not really my drug of choice. I'm more of a rum and black man myself.'

She hesitated, took another drag. Thin magenta lines traced in outline the bush, the blades of grass lit from the house, the man's profile; an odd cry came from overhead, as if a seagull had strayed too far inland. Her attention, pulled in such disparate directions, fought for to focus on a question, an utterance of any kind. Then it came to her to ask, 'So how come you have a spliff on you?'

He cleared his throat and lay back on his elbows. 'Interesting story. I bumped into some yuppie on my way in who said he borrowed £50 from me ten years ago. It sounded unlikely, but crazier things have happened. I told him to give me whatever he had, and he gave me a stick of tea. Then I saw the disco and I split.' Again his laugh stirred something in her, and now she knew why. He wasn't laughing because he was off his face or from a social reflex, because everybody else was laughing. His laughter was authentic; he was genuinely amused. 'I couldn't face it – I walked straight out the door again.'

'You left the party? So how did you get into the garden?'

'I had a change of heart and climbed over the gate,' he said, 'don't ask me why.' He took a hipflask from his jacket pocket and put it to his lips. 'I must have known you were waiting for me,' he said in a tone of mock seduction, touching her hand with his fingertips. 'Whoever you are.'

Context was everything, she realised, stoned as she was. If it weren't for the joint, the almost total absence of light and the fact of her wedding anniversary, this stranger's fingers on the back of her hand would have made no impression – would have been trivial, irritating, instantly forgettable. As it was, the brief moment of contact set off a chain reaction that ended between her thighs. When he lit a cigarette, for an instant she caught a glimpse of an aquiline nose, a high forehead and full lips.

'I can't fuck you,' she said, 'but I can suck you.'

He exhaled slowly, appearing to consider her offer as a first approach in a long negotiation. 'You know,' he said at last, 'I don't think we're destined to be lovers.'

'What an elegant brush-off.' A drawling wail came from the depths of the house, as if someone had trodden on someone's toe to cut short some sarcastic riposte.

'I'm not brushing you off, as such. I see us more as intellectual companions, that's all.'

'Already? You already see that?'

'Yes, already. Can't you tell? We chime sweetly together. We ring them bells.'

'You might want to talk to me and fuck me as well. How can you say until you know what I look like?' Laura sat up and took the cigarette from between his fingers. 'For all you know, I could be the love of your life.'

'Oh, I doubt that very much.' She drank again from his hipflask, tasting rum and blackcurrant, as warm as the spring night and grounding after the dizzying smoke. She gave it back, the hipflask, and their fingers locked, but he was somewhere else. 'You see, I met her last night – the love of my life, I mean. Oh my God.' He sat bolt upright, coughing on his smoke.

'What?' said Laura, startled, sitting up herself and then collapsing on her side, quite incapable of any sensible motion.

'Everything she wore was *black*. Bra, stockings, knickers, that thing in her hair, her chignon. Rayon, spandex, acrylic, zylon – all black.'

She tried and failed again to raise herself; the earth dragged her down. 'Jesus, what are you, some kind of textile fetishist?' He fell back on the soil, laughing, while she flailed. 'I don't want to talk about your girlfriend,' she said. 'Let's talk about something else.'

A commotion sounded from the open windows above, as if a flock of flamingos had landed in a cartload of macaques, although it was probably just some joker jitterbugging on a coffee table. Laura felt a spasm of anxiety for her husband, in there fending for himself. Alberto could do bravado, but not very well and not for very long. But then the guy with the laugh nudged her knee with his hipflask, and she forgot about Alberto. Only then did it strike her that she could hang on to his flask and make him wrestle, that wrestling for his hipflask might be the way to his heart. She took a slug and hid it behind her back.

'So do you spend every night wandering around London and picking up stray women?'

'Ha! Only in my dreams. Last night I got lucky.'

'So last night was different.'

'Last night was scary.'

'Of course,' she said, releasing the flask to him in a moment of supreme absentmindedness. 'The bomb.'

'I was quite close when it went off. I heard somebody scream.'

He took back the flask and drank in silence. Heat rose from the ground; a thousand particles of shame and an odd kind of happiness rose in her blood. She was in love with this moment, with the way he withheld, with the flavours of rum and smoke. Letting herself fall, she felt beneath her back the hot earth spin on its axis and saw herself on a dark globe turning in the sky. She wouldn't have called herself romantic, but she liked her men to be starry-eyed, to drink wine in the morning and eat breakfast at night. She often met guys in bars and business meetings and on the riverbus when she cruised, studs and stags and fanny rats who dressed themselves up to look dreamy but were far from it. She could spot a charlatan at a hundred paces – but this one was for real.

Taking his flask, she drank until it was light and wiped her lips with the back of her hand. 'We can be intellectual companions,' she said, 'if that's what you want. But I guess you have a lot of them already.'

'I used to, but none of them seem to want to talk to me anymore. What about this husband of yours? Where is he, anyway?'

'Alberto? He's in there somewhere,' she gestured with her thumb towards the house. 'He's very intelligent, if that's what you mean. But he has to be intelligent all the time, even when I want him to be stupid.'

She sensed that her real thing was about to leave; she didn't want him to go, but she had no way to keep him. She wished for a pen and paper and with her free hand found a twig and began to scratch her number in the dirt. He stood, brushing the dust from his trousers and reaching down for his flask; she handed it up but remained where she was, pinned to the ground by a terrible weakness in her lower body.

'So tomorrow,' he said, 'let's meet.'

'Tomorrow is Sunday.'

'So while your husband's in church we can have us some clever talk or be stupid together, whichever comes natural.'

He began to walk away across the lawn, his sloping figure lit briefly from the house before passing into a further patch of shadow. She called out after him, sounding to herself like a gull calling through the hot spring air, 'Are you going to tell me where?'

He stopped by the garden gate; his voice came out of the darkness. 'You're the player – you name the place.'

'The Windmill,' she said, 'on Clapham Common. But how will we know each other?'

'Well, that's the test.' He laughed again – and then he was gone, with a creak and a slam. Laura closed her eyes. A siren wailed from Shepherds Bush Green, a firework exploded a street away; airplanes descended on Heathrow, one after another, making the air vibrate, while *Wonderwall* shook the window frames of the little mansion.

She stood, then fell to her knees. 'Goodnight,' she called after him, scrambling in the loose cuttings. 'Goodnight,' she echoed herself, 'goodnight.'

She lay where she was for a while, collecting herself, before crossing to the terrace, where she saw in time her husband's back through the open kitchen door. He stood at ease in his moleskin trousers, a tin of Stella in his hand – keeping in with his host and hostess, although they talked to each other as if he wasn't in the room.

'I thought Dean might come tonight,' the hostess was saying, 'but he seems to have dumped us.'

'Just in the nick of time,' laughed the host,' before we dumped him.' Alberto turned, peering out into the night, and Laura shrank back into the shadows. 'It's strange how reclusive he's become,' said the host. 'Do you remember when you couldn't have a party without him?'

'Not a real party, at any rate,' agreed the hostess. 'He was like our Black Prince, wasn't he?'

'I wonder,' Alberto spoke up suddenly, 'has anyone seen my wife?'

'Now *that* was the kind of question people used to ask at a Dean Russler party,' said the host. 'What does she look like?'

'It was our wedding anniversary,' she heard Alberto say. 'Our fifth,' he added, irrelevantly. Laura fought off the instinct that would have dragged her into the room. 'She's in a dress, black chiffon and purple taffeta. Blonde,' he said, 'blue eyes.'

'Oh, he means Laura, you silly,' the hostess said to the host. 'I saw her go out into the garden. Actually, that was ages ago.'

'She must have fallen asleep under a bush.'

'Our wooden wedding, and she falls asleep under a bush.'

This time nobody laughed, and in a heartbeat the hostess went back to her previous topic. 'Did I tell you? I bumped into him a week or so ago in Old Compton Street and he seemed disgusted with the lot of us, said what were we anyway but a bunch of merchant bankers.'

'But that's just ridiculous,' said the host, 'when he could have been one himself. He just thought he was too special to do what the rest of us did.'

The hostess shook her icecubes and laughed. 'Dean in the fast stream, really? He was always going to end up as some Lothario with an overdraft. You know he's actually a filing clerk – can you believe it? He's been temping in an office somewhere near Victoria. The person, I mean, not the place. All that expensive education, and all he ever needed was his ABC.'

The room filled up at that moment, and the hostess dug out a box of white wine and began to fill glasses. Laura found one empty by her feet and walked into the kitchen; she knew by the way they turned to stare that her hair must be full of last year's leaves. Without looking at her husband, she held out her glass and watched her hostess fill it with chardonnay.

# Writing to Estelle

On Sunday morning, Dean was woken at dawn by the nurse who lived on the floor above. She had a regular schedule at the end of every nightshift, announcing her return in a slamming of doors, playing a single song at top volume then throwing herself on her bed. This morning the song was *Live Forever*, turned up so loud that he almost caught the whispered 'Yeah' at the beginning. Dean hated Oasis, and hated this song in particular for its phony uplift and false bravura – but lying at first light in the well of noise it created, he felt sorry for a tune that time would one day leave stranded, which would grow into an old ditty whose audience were too fucked to fuck to its simple rhythms.

When he woke again it was breakfast time. He was tempted to start his day with a glass of leftover wine, and ventured into the kitchen to uncork an unfinished bottle of Pinot Noir. But then he stood for a moment, mesmerised by the view through the small window that looked from the back of the flat beyond fire escapes and Romeo cages towards the source of all the bells that peeled through the morning. The city summer hovered in a space somewhere over Euston, an urgent amalgam of sight and sound, like something with its own purpose that at the same time gave him carte blanche. But he changed his mind about the wine, and left the kitchen with a cup of cold coffee that he found sitting on the side, then sat at his desk in the front room and picked up his pen to write to Estelle – these days his only correspondent.

Chère Estelle,

This morning I have stalked about my flat, discovering in its dusty corners a collection of insect eggs, a small plastic barrel of rum, a tennis shoe, the first House of Love LP on cassette, a back issue of the TLS and a sprig of rosemary – a forgotten gift from Ophelia. My windows face north, but even so the light pours in, and on a morning in late spring my front room glows like a cathedral in Italy, albeit one whose aisles are filled with the bric-a-brac of a half-hearted consumerist.

He put down his pen and relit his cigarette. From his desk he saw through the grubby pane down into the street, where a ragbag figure staggered into view and came to a halt at the corner of Camden Street, a scrawny blonde with an uncanny resemblance to Judee Sill. He remembered talking to her at the bar in Dolly Fossetts a year or so ago. This morning she dragged along the pavement behind her a hessian sack filled with God knew what, an unwashed spray of thin hair stuck to her shoulders, her owlish spectacles askew on lumpy cheekbones. Letting go of her burden for a moment, she stood at the kerb and gesticulated at her own shadow, a dark wraith spilling into the gutter. Odd syllables of her jerky expostulations floated up through a grind of buses and revving motorcycles, audible even through the closed window.

As you were always so keen to point out, at times I bought into the acquisitive culture that flourished under Thatcher. It is true that even on my limited budget I have acquired things – and today they lie around me in my two rooms of gloom, my mountains of comics and shelves of vinyl. My turntable was once a good one, though today its platter wobbles from too many house moves. I have a bookcase full of books in my bedroom and another in what passes for a living room. Other than that, I have no savings or assets of any description. But you would not believe me when I said that I liked it that way.

He stopped writing again to watch the bag lady dispute with her own skinny shade, and thought of going down to help in some way, maybe give her someone to shout at who was not her own shadow – but he was unwilling to interrupt his flow. As it was, he'd lost his train of thought, and when he read through what he'd written he wasn't sure what he was aiming for, or why. Estelle was the last woman he'd hooked up with for long enough to be called a girlfriend. She was a hippy chick, earnest and gauche, openly embarrassed by his antiquity at times. She was much too young for him, of course – but they were altogether a bad fit; she was mean to him, he was mean to her back. One night he'd told her that the name Estelle was wasted on the girl Estelle, and she'd walked away from him crying. But the beginning had been sweet, memorable: in their first few weeks together they'd lie on top of each other in parks across the city and he'd whisper in her ear, 'Stella, Stella for star.' In the end they fell apart quite naturally – ceased upon the midnight with no pain, as he put it in his diary, at a bus stop in Elephant and Castle.

Down in the street, a guy in cowboy boots emerged from nowhere, walked up to Judee Sill, spoke to her for a minute then hoisted her hessian sack on his shoulder. The two of them went off up Camden Road side by side, talking away – Judee and a cowboy with nothing better to do than to help a sad lady with her sackful of woes. This was what Dean loved about Camden, this louche union of acid casualties, smackheads and drunks, some curly but some straight enough to step up, like one long

47

enactment of fallen wayfarers and good Samaritans, all of them on something.

The thread was certainly lost now – but it was his morning's task and he went back to it, almost stabbing the letter with his pen.

> Thatcher ruined my life. There, I have said it. But I always thought this a hard concept to grasp for someone as young as you. I recollect with surprising clarity the three-day week, Wilson resigning out of the blue and our winter of discontent, even if I was only knee-high to a grasshopper for the first of those and as tall as a Shetland pony for the last. Oh best of Estelles, you and I do not really disagree when it comes to politics. It was just that you could not live with my scepticism, just as I could not live with your opinion of me as a material boy, in denial of the gossamer strands that bind our universe. Of course, you never saw my flat – more a hovel in mid-air than an apartment, full of impoverished ghosts and me, their penniless offspring.

He put his pen down and put his head in his hands; shades of the previous evening fell across his morning mood, flitting before his inner eye. The air was terribly close, and after a minute he got up and thrust open the window, which sank back again straightaway on its broken sash. So he grabbed from the pile of books at his feet the *Rough Guide to*

*Belgium & Luxembourg* and stuck it in the gap. This slim tome had been filched from Waterstones in a moment of sincere madness; when he slipped it into his satchel, he'd honestly believed he'd plan a trip, take in some Hanseatic sites – but the intention barely outlasted the fleeting thrill of shoplifting. Why go anywhere, after all, when he could take his trips within the six zones of the capital? What could the Grand Tour signify to someone who lived in this serpentine network of streets and waterways, among these sparkling towers and subterranean passageways?

Again he was drawn back to his morning task – but when he read through his pompous yet meagre sentences, they seemed so out of sync with reality that he almost tore the whole thing up. Where was she, where was he in all those words? Where was she, in fact, full stop? When he let himself think about it, he realised that he had no idea of Estelle's address; the last he knew of her was that she'd moved out of her boxroom in Brixton and was sleeping on people's sofas. And he felt bad when he thought about it, because she could have stayed with him – he had no sofa, not even much of a chair, but he did have a bed. Then he recalled how he'd gone through exactly this thought process the last time he tried to write to Estelle: his words were too unreal, he had no address for her, he should have let her stay.

He picked up his pen once more, and was about to set out on a sentence that would make this a new and different kind of communication – he'd think of how to get it to her once he'd sealed the envelope – when a breeze sucked the letter from under his hand. The sheet of paper was borne swiftly across the mountain of debris on his desk; he made a grab for it, but it sailed out through the narrow gap of his open window, and he could only watch it float down to the pavement, where the sudden breeze as quickly died and the letter became lodged in the bars of a drain.

Ah, but this was funny, and for several minutes he laughed while tears ran down his cheeks, swaying back and forth in his chair, until all at once he stopped laughing, unable suddenly to put a finger on what had been so funny, and went over to the flimsy shelves that held his vinyl. He took out an old 12 inch, turned his amp up to a volume that wouldn't wake the nurse but was loud enough to swing – and then he swung, whirling a dervish around the filthy mandala on his landlord's carpet, spinning on the spot to Simple Minds as they sang *Someone Somewhere in Summertime*. He closed his eyes and let the song lift him to the rooftops – below he saw people burn for one another in the dark avenues of nameless estates – and when the drums came in he leapt from side to side, just as he had half a lifetime ago, back in the lost domain of the 1980s.

It was hard to tell, really, to what extent Maggie Thatcher had ruined his life, but he had nothing but affection for the era when she'd held sway, that era of his teens when he'd begun his solitary walks across the Dulwich heartlands in search of glamour. Perhaps the epoch was really as glitzy and hollow as everyone claimed, but he remembered it as a series of private dances with girls in gothic get-ups and others disguised as Princess Diana, wild and innocent and smeared in messy lippy, who guzzled Thunderbird on Friday nights and necked in carparks, giggled when they pissed themselves on the Underground, ran out of clean underwear and sprayed their socks with Impulse. The present decade, on the other hand, had puzzled him from the start; he'd felt forever out of step. If he dabbled in ecstasy it only made him sob when he came down – and it never felt right for him to throw shapes in a field, surrounded by a heaving horde who flashed their dayglo smilies, immune to pain like the Bionic Man.

When the song was over he went to his bedroom and picked up his chinos from the floor, dug out his cream turtleneck and put on his Docs. But standing fully dressed in his living room, he found himself at a loose end. The day seemed so immense in its freedoms: twelve empty hours lay ahead of him before the waitress got off her shift. Would she let him in again, he wondered. Would she even know who he was when she saw him again?

Only then did he recall the woman from the party last night. She'd flung herself at him and he'd turned her down, the sort of perverse gesture he was prone to when stoned. In fact, he remembered little about her besides her heady fragrance, a blend of alcohol, Chanel and something else, like a whiff of burning stubble. The hay was what had held him back, perhaps; there was something country about her, and he'd never felt at home in the country. But they'd hit it off, he also remembered that – and since it was roughly in the right direction for his later date, he thought he might as well keep their rendezvous.

He went down into the street, into the muggy air. Camden was in its high noon phase, crawling with crazies and delirious with derelicts. He opted for the bus, whose sedate progress would match his mood. A lone butterfly made hazy tracks ahead of him to the stop on the high street, where he rested his aching head against graffiti tags and pasted flyers in the shelter until a wired twentysomething with a guitar and goatee appeared and began to punch the timetable in time to his Walkman. Stepping away, he almost fell into the path of a shirtless adolescent who flew by on a skateboard; he stumbled as if swept up for an instant in some strange dance, catching the eye momentarily of a guy in a turquoise tank top who slouched against the wall of The Black Cap across the road. The guy caught his eye but didn't give him a second look – he could only ever make it in the straight world.

For a full minute he was in love with all these disparate elements, all so extraordinarily alive and all just about to die. The hot air smouldered with a stench of dogshit, ketchup and fortified wine and rang with sirens, backfiring bangers and black boys on mopeds, who took off suddenly at the lights with a roar and made everything shake. Running along at the back of these drumrolls and blasts of pure noise was a wheedling, broken melody; he wasn't sure where it came from at first, until he spotted the shoeless Irishman who lay flat on his back on the kerb, slowly falling into the road while he blew on his penny whistle. These were the grace notes that made it so real – this was the cadenza, the melody that strung it all together.

A minute later and the effect had entirely gone; all that was left was an everyday cacophony. Now and then he'd considered moving somewhere less frenetic, a place with one or two quiet spaces – Finsbury Park, perhaps, or Stoke Newington. But there were Camden people and Stokey people, just as there were eighties people and nineties people, and it was too late to change allegiance now. He was as attached to Camden as Camden was attached, in the form of yesterday's papers, smears of motor oil, dead flowers and yoghurt tub lids, to the old man who lay whistling in the gutter.

## Sad Paradise

Clapham Common was just as trashy as Camden Road, but there was nothing bohemian about its lonely expanse of scrubby grass. Off to one side stood the Holy Trinity Church, forbidding in its plainness and surrounded by crows. Further on was a dirty pond, and beyond it the pub where the woman from the party had said to meet. She hadn't mentioned a time, but thinking that she surely wouldn't be there as early as noon he wandered the concrete paths that divided parallelograms of patchy grass, looking for an unbroken bench. Every one of them had at least one slat missing. At first repelled by all this dreariness, by the time he'd walked the equivalent of a block and stood in front of The Windmill, his repulsion had mutated into a species of respect for Clapham's shameless mediocrity.

By now it was lunchtime, and when he came back out front with his pint of Directors he found the tables rapidly filling. He chose one near the fringes, took out his book and cigarettes and bent his head over the page. A little Sunday traffic dribbled by; the pub forecourt was filled with human voices, chiming their secular concerns to the four winds. Dean did his best to ignore the querulous duo who sat at the other end of the table. Of his own vintage but with the air of an older couple, they bickered with winsome facility about everything under the sun. Now and then they glanced over at him pityingly, seeing him without a mate – a tragic thing indeed for a man of a certain age on the sabbath.

He looked back to his book, Kerouac's *Subterraneans*. As his eye ran over its ornate riffs, he thought about the waitress – she came back to him in flashes, like someone coming and going from a room and turning the light on and off. He'd try to see her tonight; nothing might come of it, she might not want to let him in when he rang her bell. But if she didn't, someone else would be lying in wait for him on his ride home. This was what he'd told himself on similar occasions over the years – and there'd certainly been one summer, a long time ago, when it was almost true. He'd taken that summer and multiplied it in his mind and arrived at his vision of abundance.

He was about halfway through his pint when he became aware of someone sitting across from him; he looked up to find a pair of eyes gazing into his own, betraying a curiosity both satirical and sincere. To judge by the small amount of wine in her glass, she must have been sitting there for quite a while without his noticing. She was his mirror image, with a cigarette in one hand, held between long and almost mannish fingers, and her other hand holding down the pages of a book.

They allowed each other a moment of quiet study. She was not his type – one of those long and bony Englishwomen who look out of place in anything other than a ballgown. This one wore a dress of citron yellow cotton with a pattern of little brown crocodiles from hem to hem. Fine blonde hair fell across her face, getting in the way of her large blue eyes. They were English eyes, open to the world but unmarked by all the trouble they'd seen, washed clear every spring by some internal rain.

'I think we passed the test,' she said at last, and raised her glass.

'Ah,' he said. 'Now I understand.'

'What do you understand?' She looked away and took a drag on her cigarette before glancing across at the couple at the end of the table. 'Are you still stoned?'

'Do you even know who I am?'

She laughed, shooting smoke in his direction. 'But of course. How could I fail to recognise the infamous Dean Russler?' She stubbed out her cigarette and with ironical courtesy held out her hand. 'I'm Laura Carbonaro.'

He took her hand without thinking. His mind was taken with the sound of her voice, a clear and airy sound that administered a cure to his aching head, made him feel less icky under all that low cloud. He dropped his eyes and picked up his pint. 'I'd better drink up before it goes tepid.'

'Yes,' she said, 'drink up and I'll get you another.'

She watched him drink so intently that downing his pint had the flavour of a performance. He bowed in his seat at the finish and, in imitation, she lifted her spritzer and polished it off with a flourish, making him laugh. The couple at the end of the table looked over, their pity turning green. He winked at them and held out his empty glass to Laura, who began to rise; but then she sat down again.

'It's strange how often I've heard your name,' she said, 'but never clapped eyes on you till now.'

'Sheer serendipity. You meet me at a crucial moment,' he said, watching two pigeons peck the same bread roll on the margins of the forecourt. 'A significant juncture in my life.'

He could see that she didn't believe him. 'What would you normally be doing on a day like this?'

'Me?' He met her eye, a cool blue thing in the hot afternoon. 'I make a point of doing nothing on a Sunday. Sundays are superfluous, supernumerary. As far as I'm concerned, the week has only six days in it.'

His sermon seemed to drag, but he was waiting for her to go and fetch him a drink. Instead, she fixed her eyes on the cover of the novel she was reading – she'd placed it face down on the table, something chunky by Iris Murdoch. 'What a waste of our one day of rest,' she murmured. 'Of course, I'm not *deeply* religious myself.' She blew smoke over the heads of their neighbours, who'd gone very quiet. 'But I like a man to follow a tradition of some sort. If your Sundays are so blank, why not write a book?'

Dean saw that he'd undersold himself; he would have to correct the impression that he was merely indolent. 'Oh, I write all the time.' He picked up his pint glass and gazed into the dregs, thinking of the letter that had blown out of his window that morning. 'You should see my collected works.'

Laura stood and held out her hand for the glass. He gave it to her, rising in his seat for a moment, then watched her stride away across the dull cement, her dress tracing the lines of her hips. When she returned with their drinks, they resumed their introductions, holding a tête-à-tête in a quiet clearing while around them Clapham drinkers bellowed and brayed.

'So what about you?' He sipped gratefully at his fresh pint. 'What would you normally do on a Sunday?'

'Sometimes I have a lie-in,' she said, 'and sometimes I go with my husband to Mass. Then I tend to draw things while he works on his articles. Alberto is an academic. At least, that's what he wanted to be when he was younger.' She rubbed the tip of her nose and twirled the stem of her glass so that the icecubes made a kind of music. 'He still plays at it, sends little things off to journals. No,' she interrupted herself, '*plays* is the wrong word. My husband is a very serious man, Dean.'

'And where is your husband this afternoon?'

'He has some sort of get-together with the guys from work.' Laura cleared her throat and looked heavenwards. 'Alberto has many jobs, I've lost count of how many he has. He works all night and all day, and he's still not rich.'

'Won't he get home and miss you?'

She rolled her eyes. 'Oh, I dare say I shan't see him until the early hours. That crowd have a little cocaine thing going.'

'Really?'

'You sound disapproving, Dean.' She laughed somewhat throatily; the couple upwind of them hung on every word.

He shrugged. 'It's not my drug of choice.'

'You seem less spiky than you did last night,' she observed. 'There was something almost hostile about you, but oddly attractive all the same.'

'I just couldn't see very much,' he reminded her. 'My spikiness, as you call it, was a form of protection.'

'Perhaps it was, but I liked it nonetheless. Poor Alberto has no spikes at all, and it does him no good. Something knocked his confidence a couple of years ago and he's turned into this withered intellectual. At least sometimes he used to read the poetry – now all he thinks about is Lucrezia Borgia's bank account and how much pocket money Dante gave Beatrice. Of course,' she smiled at the eavesdroppers, 'I love him dearly. He's my husband, after all.'

'So how come you got married? You don't really seem the type.' Dean had never met such an unwifely wife, but he could hardly say so in front of their audience.

'That was why, really. No one expected me to marry, so I thought I'd surprise them all. These gestures never have the effect you intend.' She looked at him in silence for a moment. 'What about you? Has there ever been a Mrs Russler?'

'God has other plans for me.'

'Clever old God,' she laughed. Suddenly she reached up with her palms towards the sky, where sun had burnt off the haze. 'I know it's perverse, but I love London on these hot spring days when you can hardly move for being drenched in sweat.'

'Yes,' he said, 'I do too. Perhaps we're both cold-blooded.'

'Perhaps we are,' she said, meeting his eye again. 'Would you like to finish your drink and go for a stroll? Around the Long Pond, such as it is.'

And so they strolled around the concrete perimeter of the Long Pond, smoking and talking and touching only now and then by accident, when their elbows met in mid-air or they grazed hips. She moved on her long legs with an awkward grace, and in her slipstream the swelter seemed less ferocious. Their promenade with only words between them had something old-fashioned about it; she was funny and clever, and he enjoyed her company, her contrapuntal style and her interest in him, which seemed mainly cerebral. But his concentration wavered as his mind went back to his date with fate, to his waitress.

They came to a halt in front of a duck, which glanced expectantly from one to the other of them, making a point with its beak. Searching his pockets, Dean remarked on how little London had changed in the wake of the bombs that spring. 'Nothing ever seems to leave a mark on this city,' he said. 'I mean, buildings rise and fall and all the rest of it, but London is such chaos that the odd gap here and there makes bugger-all difference.'

'Hmm, maybe. People look a bit more nervous than usual, don't you think?'

'But shouldn't they be looking a *lot* more nervous? Some jerk from Hampshire goes around blowing up the streets where they live and work and they all just groove on as if there was no tomorrow.'

'It's been that kind of decade,' said Laura. 'Groovy.'

Dean found in his pocket the end of a Twix and threw it vaguely at the duck, where it sank beneath the oily surface. 'A happy hell and a sad paradise.' He turned to find Laura, hand on her hip, laughing silently. 'But what kind of wanker would want to blow up a random bunch of people he doesn't even know?'

Laura walked on and he followed. 'So you'd be happier with all this if the people he killed had been his personal enemies?'

'I would, actually. Blowing up a total stranger is so futile and inhuman. There's something genuinely tragic about killing someone you hate.'

They went on a few paces; then she stopped again, took his cigarette from his fingers and drew on it hard. 'And you like a bit of a tragedy, don't you Dean? You think it kind of decorates a scene, Dean.' She giggled, flicking the fag-end over his shoulder, barely missing his ear.

Her long, cool figure seemed to extend in the heat – and for an instant he saw himself grappling her to the ground or throwing her into the pond, not out of rage or anger but just as something to do. 'I don't do the universal empathy gig, if that's what you mean.'

'And what about you? How would you feel about someone taking a strong dislike to you and planting a bomb in your satchel?'

'Oh,' he said, 'that kind of thing doesn't faze me. I mean, I'm not afraid that something bad will happen to me – I'd be more scared of the same good thing happening again and again.'

The duck gave up on the Twix and headed instead for the bobbing butt. Seeds fell like parachutes all around the stagnant pool, as if nature had made an air drop; they drifted to the centre of the water, then were lifted up and away by a breeze he couldn't feel. Laura, quiet beside him, seemed to be watching the same phenomenon, but Dean had learned not to trust the illusion of a shared vision. If he threw her in the pond, would she sink or float – and if she floated, what would it prove? She stooped to put back on her low-heeled shoes, which she'd taken off for their stroll, despite the plethora of turds and splinters of broken glass.

'I'd better go,' she said. 'Poor Alberto will think I'm having an affair.'

'I thought he was off doing his cocaine thing.'

'Oh, I just say these things to make him sound more interesting. Alberto wouldn't know cocaine from caster sugar.'

They said their goodbyes and he watched her walk away across the Common, a long pale line weaving in shimmering heat. They were bound to meet again, he thought. As they walked, they'd shared the kind of titbits new friends nibble from a lack of mutual knowledge – but even those trivial subjects seemed lively on her lips. She had a sexy cortex, a cleverness almost erotic, and something in her view of him seemed to jibe with a view of himself lost in the ten ignominious years since leaving university, a decade of telemarketing, audio typing and data input. She somehow brought back to him the fact that once he'd wanted it all: to browse for hours in the world's greatest library, bask in a glade in the Forest of Arden, hide behind drums all night at the Camden Falcon and wake each morning to a lovebite from Cleopatra or Lilith or Helen of Troy. He'd wanted to encompass all knowledge, experience every sensation. People who bothered to look saw only his bumbling attempts to make ends meet – they had no suspicion of his stellar ambitions. But then he'd forgotten them himself until this afternoon, when Laura Carbonaro had jogged his memory.

When he looked for her again, she'd vanished into the backdrop of red buses and redbrick houses, leaving him alone on the Common's parched and sordid spread. So he left it and sat for a couple of hours outside a wine bar on Venn Street, reading his book until it was time for an early evening showing of *American Beauty* at the Picturehouse – then emerging into the ends of twilight, he took a bus to Streatham Hill.

## Laura's Dilemma I

After parting from Dean, Laura went home to her terraced house in a street not far from the Common. She wandered the rooms, arranging her thoughts, but in every bright doorway she came face to face with her husband. He confronted her with doleful eyes, doing his best millstone impression. So she retreated to her studio on the pretext of work, stuck her hand inside her dress and brought herself off. Fantasising her own fingers as someone else's tongue was a feat beyond her imagination, and the pleasure it brought was faint and indistinct – but this afternoon she settled for that last resort, since

66

coming to a climax seemed the only proper response to her feelings.

While she masturbated at her drawing board with her knickers around her ankles, she thought about her new acquaintance. He had interesting eyes, darkish brown and slightly demonic, a high forehead from which hair had begun to disappear and a mouth that went from sullen to smiling in an instant. He had no great aura around him and few other distinguishing features, yet she saw in him an opportunity to make amends to herself for some of her more egregious life choices. After a couple of minutes of idle fiddling, she came with a small bang and slid partway from her chair. Then she sat up, licked her fingers and began to sketch the image of his penis, as it might look when erect. She drew it over and again, experimenting with length and density – a foolish occupation for a Sunday afternoon, but at least it gave her time to reflect on the events of the weekend.

It was hard to believe that she and Alberto had been married for five years – but then most things were hard to believe, if you thought about them for too long. She remembered him in New York, courting her on a night out at the Village Vanguard, a day on the Ferris wheel at Coney Island, a morning eating bagels in Sheepshead Bay. He'd been her Little Italy, her brainy Don. When she wrote to her mother with news about her new male discovery, her mother wrote back with a specific instruction that just begged to be ignored. 'Don't do anything stupid, darling,' her mother's letter said – but who ever listens to their mother? A year later she married him, with scant blessings but with a mischievous look on what her new husband called her 'doll face'.

It was strange to think back on that courtship now, when the thought of being courted made her feel slightly nauseous. To be the target for honeyed words and grand gestures, to be made to feel unreal in the name of romance, a medieval scene with its cardboard swords and papier-mâché armour – she'd take a wide detour these days to avoid such a fate. Dean would do none of those things; he wasn't the courtly kind. In Camelot he would have written pornographic odes to Guinevere then conjured her up in the confines of the little boys' room. He would take no pains over her – she'd have to buy her own guitar, find a balcony and do all the serenading – but that was part of his attraction. She only wanted him to respond with vigour to some of her more preposterous suggestions.

Laura stood and rearranged her garments, then rubbed furiously at her doodles with a rubber until she realised that her sketches of tumescent dicks were too deeply engraved to be erased. She grabbed the sheet from her drawing board, but hesitated at the point of throwing it away. Instead she turned it over, to shield her graffiti from prying eyes, then went downstairs to cook her unhappy bunny an early dinner.

Laura Carbonaro was a mass of contradictions. She liked furniture and sex, but she liked mental things too, the life of the mind. Her personality was composed of elements she'd chosen to emphasise from an early age, when she decided that to get the most out of life she should act with maximum perversity. She went against sense and reason whenever it seemed right; she wasn't predictably perverse but oscillated between capriciousness and normal behaviour so that no one, not even herself, knew which Laura they'd get. Even as a young girl she'd realised that she must truly inhabit her role to make it convincing, that her weird predilections and bizarre decisions must smack of authenticity, so that over time she became the person she appeared to be – and the 'real' Laura, or whoever she might have been instead, was lost forever.

In the five years of her marriage, she'd got together with a dozen other men she'd picked up in bookshops, taxi queues and dentists' waiting rooms. Her husband's reactions to these infidelities had diminished to a point when his distress was barely detectable. On the first occasion when she stayed out all night, wrapped in the arms of an Australian barman she'd lured and cosseted outside the Kensington Olympia, Alberto even threatened to kill himself on the morning of her return. She questioned his ability to do anything so visceral – but really she didn't want him to die; she enjoyed the stability and status that marriage conferred, liked having someone around to Hoover while she cooked.

Feeling listless after her insubstantial orgasm, she put a pinch of garam masala in the sauce, dipped into the pickle jar and stained the rice with turmeric with an air so absent that her husband couldn't fail to notice. He said he wanted to help, then hovered mournfully by her side and did very little except stir the pot. Looking up from the chopping board, she found his sad eyes fixed on the hem of her dress; she smiled at him and he smiled back, sadly, then slammed the heel of his hand into a clove of garlic.

After all, there was no end to the things that Alberto could fail to notice. When he no longer threatened suicide but was merely ironic at the discovery of her latest exploit, she'd explicitly

directed him to make the most of his Latin charms
– but, as far as she knew, his absurdly high IQ had
won him no friends between the sheets. She might
have given him lessons in body language and lines
to say, but she had no faith in his ability to learn.
Oh, he was a hopeless case, her poor Alberto!

# Capital Gold

For those weeks from the start of May into
midsummer, Dean and Monika rarely left her room.
Whenever she wasn't working he shared her small
space and her disregard for anything that lay
beyond its four walls. Sometimes they went as far
as the lounge, done up many aeons ago, when dirty
biscuit and fusty taupe were the only colours in the
rainbow. Now and then they relaxed on the sagging
settee, staring at the blank screen of a battered
television that no one ever turned on and for which
no one had a licence – his eye drawn instead to an
Athena poster of a nervy-looking tiger, gazing
pointlessly through the fronds of a stylised
rainforest. They'd sit and smoke – he smoked with
her, although it was not his drug of choice – and talk
of nothing, while the light took an age to fade.

On the wicker coffee table in the lounge was her stash, the resin and papers and Swan Vestas filters she used for roaches, and laid over the grubby carpet underneath the table a Muslim prayer mat, which her landlord had bought in a clearance sale because he liked the crescent moon on the dome of the mosque. Now and then she knelt before the mat to pick out shreds of grass or hash blims, finding enough to make another joint. And then she'd get stoned again and she'd get him stoned, and then they'd go back to bed.

Neither of them worked regular hours – Monika had her shifts and Dean was occasionally jobless – so love might be made at almost any hour of day or night. In those precious weeks of high summer, he learned to distinguish between sex about midnight and sex at noon, fucking in the hour before dawn and their long, slow screws around twilight. Afternoons were what he loved best; the sex they had after dark was oddly formal, almost clichéd by comparison. He loved those times when they lay together at three or four in the afternoon with her window thrown open on the sounds from the street, car radios blasting Capital Gold while heat rose from the tarmac and filled her room with its tacky black scent. In that passage without milestones between midday and dusk, time lost its meaning;

they lay side by side, stopping and starting sometimes for hours while the sky dimmed until, at length, they took turns in the bathroom, that little enclave of urine and mould, so encrusted with sweat and seminal stuff that the first splash of water felt like a rebirth.

The narrowness of her existence attracted and repelled him, repelled him even though it was what he'd been looking for so long. He'd sought high and low, at least in dreams, for someone who paid as little attention as he did to the nuts and bolts of living, all those complex strategies required to make it in the superstructure that contained everything and everyone. Of course, he'd always dreamed of a woman like this, who seemed so given up to a life of the senses and whose senses seemed so often deranged. It was true that her single-mindedness gave their fucking an extraordinary ferocity: she'd tear skin from his back, chew on his nipples and gnaw at his dick with both mouths. She changed sex for him – and not just because her limbs ran so sweetly together or because she was so sensitive in all her extremities. She made love seriously, as if it were a matter of life and death, never holding back – not like other women, not like Estelle, who would always tense at the point of climax and announce her impending doom in so many words, like a

73

station announcer telling the platform about the arrival of a train. Monika needed no words and made no announcements but kept on moving into him, on and on through the last moment, until he felt he found eternity in the back of her box.

But when it was over, she retreated to a place where she didn't expect him to follow, where her eyes lost all expression – her gaze ending at the open window, through which blew in on the fumy air a nonstop symphony of screeching tyres, beeps and honks and shrieks of neighbourly rage. In the small hours while she slept, Dean lay and listened to wailings of mating cats and barking foxes and thought about sex – how with age it had become a sort of metaphysical language, even if it was spoken in low voices in low lighting, a discourse with himself on whether touch was really touch, whether anything real was really happening. Recently, on the sporadic occasions when it was offered, sex with a woman had often left him alone in his body and abandoned by desire, undesired and undesiring, like a reluctant Buddhist. But Monika had changed all that: with her, no question marks arose over the moment to punctuate his orgasms with curly heads and dotted tails. As she rolled her wet mouth in the palm of his hand and pinned him down with her mons, she undid his ties to the world of work, and

74

all those other worlds. Locked together, they floated free from a realm of mediocrity that others took for granted, the dominion of the cruel and mundane, a world where stupid Nazis planted bombs in public houses then stood off to watch them explode.

How could that not be enough? What more could he want, he often asked himself, now that his prayers had been answered. But in between fucks, her long feline trances made him uneasy. When she spoke, it was only to describe her cloudy state of mind, the endless heat, the tightness of her thong, the awfulness of her job at the casino. Her English was rather lovely; it drew attention to itself, made the language itself seem fuckable. She spoke to the point in a way that a native speaker might have found difficult, but her topics were restricted to the few activities that took place in her tiny sphere. At first he'd liked being so remote from knowing what she was thinking – it was a cheap way of preserving her mystique – but after a while her silences began to trouble him. Oh, if only she could talk! But then, if she could talk, wouldn't he just find another way to resist her, just as he'd kept at arm's length any articulate woman he'd ever known? As it was, her long moments of internal migration led him to believe that she withheld details of her life that she'd willingly tell to a member of her own tribe, or another man.

She'd never been to see him in Camden – indeed, she spoke of any place north of the river as if it were darkest Peru – but now and then he suggested it, knowing she'd say no. They rarely left the humdrum heights of Streatham Hill even for a drink or a show, and living within such narrow parameters naturally intensified their strange intimacy. In that small space he came to know her mood swings, how quickly she could break off from however she was feeling to turn sad or hilarious or enraged, sullen or absent or easily amused. In the crucial moment before they went to her room to have sex, she might glare at him as if awaiting the fatal provocation, one false move that would cause her to stub out her joint in his eye – but then as they rolled on her bed again, her face became again a map of ecstasy, an A to Z of pleasure. Just as instantly, however, in the echoes of her last climax, she'd leap from his side, curse his spunk for running down her thighs, wipe herself off with his shirt.

The approach of midsummer brought rain, but it was a hot rain, and London in the week leading up to the solstice felt as steamy as Ecuador. In all that tropical heat, his waitress seemed to recede behind the haze, hide out behind her smoke; each time they met her pupils seemed a little more dilated, her attitude more paranoid, the swing between moods more extreme. It mystified him, this way she had of switching from joy to fury to sorrow – but hadn't he always wanted to live inside a mystery?

# A World of Apples

On midsummer's eve, Dean waited for Monika in the doorway of the Dome café on Old Compton Street, watching dressy young men go by on high heels and hippies with bare feet, tourists lost in transit and pigs boiling in their uniforms. He'd coaxed her up to Soho to celebrate solstice, although she saw no point in it and had told him so. He had to face the fact that things he found beautiful often passed her by completely. But perhaps a primal urge won through in the end, to see out the longest day with whatever he was: her hanger-on, her entourage of one, her unhandy handyman. How she classed their relationship was unclear, but it was obvious he wasn't her boyfriend. She agreed to meet him – but no rendezvous with Monika was absolute; he could never be more than about 70% certain that she'd show.

As he stood and smoked and looked out through the hot rain that fell in streaks across the fractured facade of The Admiral Duncan, he felt the tension in his chest from knowing he was about to see her again. He turned his restless gaze from the entrepreneurs cycling their rickshaws through the downpour to a disparate band of ageing yuppies eating hors d'oeuvres in the Dome. Ten more minutes passed before impatience drove him out into the rain to wander the streets of Soho. She was late by only half an hour, but he couldn't just stand and wait. At the risk of missing her altogether, he zigzagged between Chinatown and Soho Square, admiring for a while the whiskies in the window of Milroys.

The downpour turned into a blizzard of hail, stones the size of marbles clattering on car roofs and awnings. A hailstorm in June, he thought, how strange! He ducked into a doorway in Frith Street – and there he came upon her, hiding from the hail, her eyes closed tight against the lowering sky and her beautiful head cocked against the doorframe of a members' club of the kind that Bacon and Freud had frequented in Soho's gilded age. She seemed to wake up when he pressed in beside her, opening her eyes and looking at him in amazement. They'd taken each other by surprise, something that hadn't happened since their first night, and in the burn of that spontaneity he kissed her face until, in the dark doorway, she took his hand and guided it down inside the waistband of her black lycra leggings. Smeared and blurry figures passed by on the pavement while he felt his way with his fingertips, and she groaned in his ear and shook and slumped against him for a minute, her hair clinging in strands to his lips. For a precious interval, her heartbeat slowed and meshed with his own. After a minute or two, she stood and faced him in a grainy light in which she resembled, as she sometimes did, a starlet from before the talkies.

'You shouldn't have done that, Dean,' she murmured, grinning up at his confusion. 'Now you've just made it worse.'

Lightheaded in the dusk, they walked back to Old Compton Street and found a cubicle in the Pollo, where he ordered a carafe of house white and two prawn cocktails. They were seated at the back, out of sight of the street and pleasure seekers rushing one way to the O Bar or the other way to Shuttleworths. Monika lit a cigarette and smiled at him across the table, over the laminated menu, through the fumes. He made sure to bask in her smiles, knowing how rapidly they could fade. How he loved and hated the quickness of her moods, which flickered through her like life itself, making her dull and bright by turns.

Then just as the food arrived she began to speak. At the start of her speech he wasn't really listening; she rarely made anything but small talk on the rare occasions they went out, and it was his habit just to watch the shapes she made with her wonderful mouth. Her face wore the same expression as ever when she mixed alcohol with sex – her cheeks were flushed, her eyes lit up. But then he became alert to her clipped consonants, realising that she was saying something new. Perhaps the weird weather had inspired her reminiscence. All she'd ever told him of herself before was that she came from Moldova – and even that she divulged with some reluctance, as if she wasn't sure what he'd do with the information. However it was, while she played with her cigarette and wine glass, locking her green eyes with his brown, she began to tell him her story. It was as if he'd momentarily become real to her – or real enough, at least, to hear the Transylvanian tragedy of her first love.

In the year of her country's independence, when she was 17, she hitched a lift from her village into town with a boy who drove a truck full of apples.

He stopped on the road for her, as strangers sometimes did, on the basis that nobody was really a stranger in their neck of the woods.

'That's how you say it, isn't it Dean? In our *neck of the woods*?' She laughed shortly at the idiom, gazed for a moment past him at the swinging door of the restaurant, then went back to her story.

She ate three of the apples that the boy had given her while he drove and they talked, but the boy ate none; he'd already eaten so many apples in his life that he was sick of them. 'But I mean really sick, sick like a dog. I bit one in half and asked him to share it with me. I held it out like this' – here she picked a leaf out of the salad and held it under Dean's nose. 'He stopped driving and threw up in a field. God, he hated the smell of those apples.'

Alex was the son of a rich orchard owner; it wasn't done, she implied, to question the source of anyone's wealth. In any case, his family were better off than hers. She went with him to market, where the two of them sold all his apples in under an hour. It was the first time he'd ever sold them all, he told her. Normally he would have a crate left over; sometimes he even threw it in a ditch on his way home and lied to his parents that either the apples or the money had been stolen from him by bandits. Monika laughed. 'Of course, there weren't so many bandits in those days. Now there are lots of them – but they steal cars, not apples. But his parents thought he was so amazing that they just believed anything he said.'

This was how she spoke English, with a sprinkling of idioms, a smattering of surprising vocabulary; it was part of her distinction. She paused, drank, lit a cigarette, and he held his breath – wanting her to go on but also not. Did he really want her to confess? A confession after all could change everything.

'He told me I was his lucky charm and that was how come he sold all the apples that afternoon. I was very shy then, Dean. I never went to parties – it was hard for me to talk to people I didn't know. He was the first person who opened me up.' She sighed and put her glass down and toyed with her neckline. 'In that way, I guess I owe him a lot.'

Alex drove her home, stopping the cart every now and then to kiss. 'But I didn't let him get any further.' She asked him in to meet her parents. He was seen as quite a catch; his family were wealthy, only keeping the farm as a kind of holiday home, their real business in the city. 'And he was very sweet when you first met him,' she said. 'People were always impressed with him at the start.' After a month or so, Monika and Alex were engaged to be married.

While she smoked another cigarette, he coloured in the details for himself of the cart with its flaking paint, a horse's matted mane, a cloudy day around the apple harvest, crowds in the town square. He saw a younger and more innocent Monika ride alongside her beau across the flatlands above the Danube – he was held rapt by her landscape of symbols where symbols still had power, all those crossroads and falling fruit and rivers on which farmers' children skated in winter and drowned when they burst their banks in spring. As the restaurant glimmered around them she talked on, unaware that there was anything mythical about these people or places.

For a year or so, Monika and her fiancé played about in the meadows of that remote outpost of eastern Europe, a place in the middle of nowhere in a country that was itself in the middle of nowhere, in a state of post-perestroika bliss. Their families wanted them to marry at once, but they saw no reason to lose their idyll for the lives of drudgery, ambition and resentment they'd seen their parents live. When their parents began to insist, they made a getaway to England, with a plan to save enough money to pay for a wedding dress, a church service and the first instalment on a small concrete box in Chisinau. 'But maybe we would have come here anyway. Everyone does in the end.'

'But you were in the vanguard,' Dean suggested, 'you were pioneers.' She shrugged, her features clouded, her eyes leached of their green. It was a sad story, he could already tell, or why would she be sitting here telling it to him?

With their student visas, they got past immigration in Dover, found work on the black and rented a tiny room. For six months they lived in squalor – and in their dank bedsit, lost in some foul corner of Willesden Green, things began to go awry. Alex was so depressed by their circumstances that he lost interest in everything; he sat staring at the want ads every morning before setting off to wash dishes. Every night they argued, every day they foraged for bargains and scraped by on scraps. Then one night they had one argument too many – 'He hit me on the head with a fruit bowl' – and split up.

The apple farmer went home, but Monika stayed on in England, too proud to show her face in the village or return with empty hands. She went on masquerading as a language student and getting by on tips. 'I could never have gone home,' she said. 'It all seemed so far away anyhow.'

She pushed away her plate and lit another cigarette, gazing across the room at the couples who ate and chattered. He saw it all now – her life's progress up to this point, her shattered faith and broken heart and a home that must feel more distant by the year. While she looked away, he imagined how she might have been in her original state, before smoke rerouted her neural pathways, before it had worn her down – her draining and senseless existence here, her haphazard choice in men. What an angel she must have been not so long ago in that year of bliss, running around the back country with a ring on her finger, lying with her lover in the pasture, parting demurely on a dirt road between their houses and going home to her tiny bedroom to throw herself down on her narrow bed.

For a weird minute, the restaurant seemed to go very still, as if all the other clientele were shushing each other, wanting to hear his response. And for a mad moment he thought of returning her intimacy, telling her every stumbling minute of his existence up to now, every bad turn, all those little failures, even if none of them was quite as sweet and complete as the one she'd just related. Maybe she would listen to him as he had listened to her, take away his story to think over, and the next time they met they'd be like two new people together, their lives rewritten in those moments of honesty. But it was no good, he couldn't open up that way; he was a closed book, born with his pages uncut.

So instead he broke the silence to joke around, making flippant remarks on the characters who sat at nearby tables – and when she glanced about abstractedly as if she saw nothing funny or saw nothing at all, he made a big deal over ordering a second carafe. He poured them both a glass and lifted his as if to toast their future, aping the role of the male in one of those happy and successful couples where a man would do such a thing unironically. *It's true that we're poor and going nowhere*, he wanted to say, *it's true we're chaotic and clueless and live a hand-to-mouth existence, but at least we can laugh about it. Here's to us!* But he stopped himself in time. She wouldn't laugh about it, he realised; she'd only be forced to reflect on how far she'd fallen – from her apple farmer to him, from an engagement to a series of one-night stands with the same fly-by-night.

He fell silent again, sipping his cold acid wine while she sat and stared at the tablecloth between them. He was taken aback by this quiet melancholy; it was as if she'd shrunk inside herself to vanishing point. He was used to her being morose or wired or whimsical, in her stoned way, when she was not carelessly jiggy or angrily paranoid. Her unusual mood unsettled him, made him start up again and witter on until she said, 'If you want me to forget about my life, Dean, you have to do better than that.'

It was still light when they left the restaurant, lighter in fact than when they went in because the clouds had all blown off. Above them was an open sky, depthless with the azure of midsummer, a blue that was always going away. Indiscriminate crowds swarmed seeking their simple pleasures, and he wished his own pleasures were as straightforward and the sky was not this blue vacuum, put there to remind him of just how empty things could get. Monika walked mutely through the throng with her arms folded across her chest, as they cut down the side of the National Gallery to wait at her bus stop in Trafalgar Square. He sensed none of the current that sometimes passed between them on nights like this, zinging through her body's taut wires, even through her clothes, so that it felt like his hair might stand on end when he touched her. Tonight the charge was dead – and he regretted they'd never borrowed a phrasebook from someone and learned some ordinary language of affection that would have let him put an arm around her shoulders.

At her bus stop they stood in silence and gazed up at Nelson on his column, where jackdaws wheeled in the dusk. She said nothing, but he knew what she was thinking; however often he corrected her, she remained convinced that the guy on top of the towering plinth was Napoleon. He understood her bewilderment – after all, how could a man of Bonaparte's renown be knocked off his pedestal by some one-armed sailor? And he understood as well something that had escaped him until now: how far he saw himself in that high-up figure with his vantage point, his amazing view of London, how good he was at lifting a telescope to his blind eye and saying, 'I see no ships.'

When the bus arrived, she pressed her way to the doors without glancing in his direction; she was not in the habit of standing in line. When he pushed in her wake and began to buy himself a ticket, she asked what he was doing.

'I'm coming home with you,' he said, ashamed of the pleading note in his voice, while the driver looked on impatiently. 'Like we said.'

'Come if you like,' she told him, 'but I'm not sleeping with you tonight.'

He got off the bus and walked quickly away, beat a retreat across the scorched grass of her contempt for him, knowing that if he persisted and besieged her, she might dismiss him altogether. He trooped north up Charing Cross Road through the fading blues of the longest day, licking her essence from his fingers, savouring her flavour as if for the last time.

# Songs of Sad Clapham

She was sure it only happened when he had nothing better planned but, through May and June, Dean sometimes turned up at her house. Laura would wine and dine him while her husband watched glumly. To his prejudiced eye, these dinner parties with no other guests and their outings to West End restaurants, the Barbican, the ICA or the Curzon Mayfair, must have looked like kinds of dates. Poor Alberto could certainly not have guessed that his wife's new friend had never once laid a finger on her.

Laura couldn't quite believe it, either. She'd got to know Dean in those weeks and knew him to be a person of rank indiscipline, who caved in to his desires at the smallest prompting; it was disheartening that in her case he seemed capable of resistance. They were more than just playmates at this stage, in that he told her things she was fairly sure he wouldn't say to anyone else, but it was important to her that they become lovers – if that was even the word. It probably wasn't the word: *lovers* covered too much, whereas she meant something specific. She felt that Dean had a secret so well hidden that nothing short of penetration could reveal it. So she pursued him with a look on her face ranging between frustration and foxiness – she gave herself those looks in the mirror, she knew how she appeared. And Dean meanwhile continued to confound her view of men as these simple beings, to whom sex was like planting a flag in a woman. She became the territory that chased the flag around, longing for occupation, while Dean looked on in amusement.

She'd never been to his flat, but she'd gone around town with him – showing him off to her friends, expecting him to perform the same tricks he did for her, when they were alone. But Dean seemed to vanish into himself as soon as they sat down with her flock of Sloanettes. She went to the bar with twitchy, button-nosed Carrie, alcoholic Tory and 'Typhoid' Mary, blousy Cathy 'Cuticles' and frowsy Annalise, and while he was out of earshot, as they waited for their bucket of ice with a bottle and glasses and he was in the bathroom, she tried to explain him. He refused to employ his talents for money, she said – he was a man out of time, an art for art's saker, an aesthete who spurned the middlebrow. But what were his talents precisely, asked Carrie and Tory, Mary and Cathy and Annalise? What evidence had Laura seen of these gifts – and how much would they be worth if he *did* try to trade them in? And then, although these were really just small things, why did he shave at all if he shaved only twice a week? Why did he never wash his shirts? And why did he have to look at them like the spawn of the devil whenever they flashed their plastic or mentioned Henley or Twickenham?

Laura's explanations didn't convince. After all, he was no sex object, or not in any obvious way, and clearly he was no substitute husband – that much was plain from the fact that she always picked up the tab. He was a conspicuous failure in the worldly sense; Alberto in comparison was a titan of overachievement. What had Dean done since leaving college? He freely told her, with a strange smirk on his face as if all his failures were only successes in disguise: he'd handed out flyers on Tottenham Court Road, taught English in various low-rep summer schools, picked strawberries in strawberry season and washed factory walls. And now he was a clerk, a clerk, and nothing but a clerk, buried in reams of A4 in a dingy office near New Oxford Street.

What drew her to him was his marginality, and the extraordinary effort he made to maintain it. She'd never met anyone who tried so hard to be so extraneous to requirements. Women whose ideal men turned up after long years of waiting would say, 'Wow, he was just what I needed!' No one would ever say that of Dean – no one would ever need him that way. Even to Laura, at the height of her passion, he was not exactly necessary. He brought her little but his never very urgent observations, his idle wit. But he had made an art of being Mr Nobody, and she loved him for it, if love was the word, loved him for keeping his secret so well. Yes, he had a secret, of that she was sure – some small, glittering thing, a dusty gem, or something more diffuse, a perfume – something he'd brought back from the nowhere he'd walked so far to reach. She wanted to be the one he told it to, and she believed that with his cock inside her, in the intimacy of that scenario, she might at least catch a glimpse.

She dared not ask what prevented her laying hands on his cock, knowing that she was far from his ideal woman – that he was turned off by her country hips and bluestocking manner, her air of middleclass prosperity. In her experience of men, even strong-minded men, such stumbling blocks would melt away soon enough, given enough alcohol and low-lit proximity. So she fed him on a variety of liquors, lit candles and sat close – but still no dice. After several failed attempts, she saw that whatever it was that stopped them lying together must be very powerful, but she tried not to make it real, aware that 'it' was really 'she'.

The drama of finding another female in her way took her into fresh territory. Laura had never been able to make herself care about what other women had, whether they'd won it through the lottery or earned it as their just desserts. Dean's advent pulled her into a new realm of possession and rivalry, but she lacked practice in the manoeuvres needed to prise a man from another woman. She was starting from a position of weakness – but she vowed to dig a tunnel, scale a wall, do anything to make him hers. At the same time she sensed that Alberto, stuck to her like a limpet since their wedding day, saw her determination and watched her from the corner of his eye.

Alberto was a problem she'd created for herself. When they married, she'd not figured on him shadowing her through life like a gloomy spectre, turning corporeal at all the worst moments. Outside the life of the mind, a narrow field whose pleasures were quickly exhausted, they had little in common. She was a sensuous woman, in love with the surface of things. In those phases of loving her house, she went from room to room, running her hands over the pea-green sofa they'd found at Heals, caressing the walnut banisters, stroking the kitchen sides; she got down on her knees and felt with her fingertips the ridges of her terracotta tiles, imported from Alberto's homeland. But Alberto hardly seemed to notice the nice things they'd bought to mark their arrival on that plateau of middleclass stability where they might spend the rest of their lives. He paid half the mortgage, but the house seemed to belong less than half to him; he walked around it as he might a public place, going from A to B without taking in a single detail.

The decay of their once bright dream of course saddened her, though not as much as his ongoing presence in her life now that the dream had died. She remembered how blithely they'd gazed into one another's eyes and said that if it worked in New York it would work anywhere. Even now, if they bickered more than usual or she was silent for a little too long, Alberto would glibly propose that they abandon everything she'd put in place. 'If it doesn't work in Clapham,' he'd say, 'maybe it would work in Chalk Farm, or Turnham Green, or Hackney Wick.' He'd say these things as they sat together in her beautiful kitchen, and she'd resist the temptation to hurl her glass at him. 'Moving can't be the answer,' she'd say instead, killing the subject. And in fact she knew she was right; she knew that he felt like a stranger in his own home, but she doubted it would be any different for him back in Penne, or any academic institution he might have ended up at in America, or wherever he might lay his hat. Alberto was one of those unfortunate men not cut out to be a nomad or a farmer, who couldn't twist or stick. Nothing about it worked anymore – but while she couldn't mend her marriage, she couldn't quite bring herself to throw it away.

Each time she came back from another frustrating evening with Dean, she expected her husband to scold her at least. But he'd only glance up at her then look back at his book – he'd be flicking through the vast tome on Piranesi she'd given him for his birthday, or poring over the *Economic History Review*, where once he'd published a short article, or she'd find him rereading Benvenuto Cellini's autobiography, his intellectual comfort blanket. This went on until a Wednesday night at the end of June, when she came in at midnight, later than usual, and Alberto had waited up. Fixing herself a mug of malted milk, she explained that she'd gone with Dean to see *Magnolia* in Leicester Square.

'Such a very long film,' she told him, mock panting as if from the exertion of sitting in a cinema seat for such ages. 'I mean it was *three hours* long.'

Alberto took a seat at the breakfast bar. 'Is that what you would say if you reviewed it for *Time Out*? Did *Dean* think it was a long film, too?' He left on her a lingering gaze, from which she read his meaning.

'My dear, we all know how you hate going to the cinema. That's why I go with other people.'

'I hate American films – that is not the same thing.'

'Well, then. So why make insinuations?' She tossed her head and burned her hand on the pan. Running it under the cold tap, she saw the London water go brown and then run clear again. Summer had already cut into the water table; the reservoir was low.

'All I am *insinuating* is that you looked at the programme, saw that the film lasted for three hours and thought that would make a good alibi for your... affair.'

Laura left the kitchen for the lounge and sat down on the pea-green couch with her milk. Alberto followed and sat beside her, sipping his cocoa. 'Oh, yes? And then what happened, my liege?'

'You got pissed and let him seduce you.'

Laura closed her eyes and wrapped her fingers around the mug. 'Dean is not interested in me in that way.'

'What a failure of taste. Not that it surprises me. English men know nothing about women. Niente di niente.'

'Thank you, sweetheart, that's nice to hear.'

'Nada,' he went on. 'Nix.'

'I get your gist, Alberto. It's the same in any language.'

'Almost,' he replied. She felt his mournful gaze on the side of her face. 'Almost the same.'


# Trysting

On the first Saturday in July, Dean came to dinner again. They dawdled over the main course, a lamb tagine, Laura's speciality. It was an evening of the sort that occurs at least once in any London summer, when the city loses itself in a game of escalating temperatures. Laura had on her cotton dress with little brown crocodiles, while Alberto wore a tie – God only knew why, at a dinner for three in his own house – and Dean his beige chinos and a white shirt with a dirty collar. He seemed exhausted, and demonstrated his exhaustion in a way that would have struck her as impolite if she hadn't been so used to him: he yawned over the nibbles and guzzled his aperitif at the start, then picked at his meat while drowning himself in Chianti. Come dessert, a scoop of icecream and blueberries, he roused himself enough to banter with Laura in what she'd come to recognise as their private language, a descent into patois that was enough to drive Alberto from the house.

After Alberto had left, Laura cleared up and moved them into the lounge. Even at six in the evening, the sun came through the bay window in a hard glare, pierced now and then by sharper arrows of light that flew in reflected from mirrors of passing cars. Dean fidgeted on the soft furnishings, looking every inch the gentleman caller – thoroughly ill at ease, as if he'd just about rather be here than anywhere else but, all the same, he didn't want to be here very much. Was it her that made him feel so uncomfortable, or was it the house?

She'd never been to his flat, but she knew him well enough to know that even his bed was rented, and that he felt at a disadvantage among the owner-occupiers of this world.

So in a while she led him out to the patio through the french windows in the kitchen. At the back of the house were two slabs of concrete and a high brick wall painted white and covered in withered wisteria. She'd planted bulbs the first year, but not much had grown, and now her back terrace only served as a reminder of what she'd left in the country.

Dean lit another cigarette from the bones of the first and turned to her with a crooked smile. 'I have a question for you, Laura.'

Sitting on a garden chair, she watched him pace her outdoor space as if it were a prison yard. In his enormous white shirt with its stained collar and sandy chinos with ash marks and burn holes, he might have been an ex-con in his first day back in his old clothes. Above them, an aeroplane made its way across patches of blue between houses, too lazy to leave a vapour trail.

'I'm listening,' she said – but warily, because Dean tended not to initiate subjects that were in any way to her advantage.

'Do you think women are ever really romantic?' He tugged at the bottom of his shirt. 'Until recently I thought they were. But now I realise they're only romantic in books – and most of those books were written by men, with one or two exceptions.'

'Weren't they all written by men though? I can't think of *any* exceptions, or not since the good old days of *Jane Eyre.*'

She kept her tone light, but his nonchalance grated. Sounds of a neighbour's TV came through an air starved of oxygen and harsh with white light, like an endless afterglow from an unending explosion. It was the last Saturday of Wimbledon; the women's final was over. Venus had won – or had she? From over the wall they heard the idle progress of mixed doubles, the pock pock pock of a rally, a scattered volley of applause.

Dean shrugged, pondering. '*By Grand Central Station I Sat Down and Wept*, if we mean novels that accept the premise of passion as a reality. But yes, it is an exception.' Setting his feet apart, he assumed a lecturing stance at odds with his overheated look. 'I suppose writers like Françoise Sagan and Margaret Drabble think of romantic love as a psychological phenomenon, or philosophical… or sociological. By and large, the only really romantic women are the creation of men.'

'I see. That's a relief to all of us, I'm sure.' Laura looked down in annoyance, smoothing the creases from the lap of her dress.

'You don't agree?'

'I know you want me to disagree.' She stood and went over to him, and without consultation began to dig around in his pocket for his cigarettes. Dean stayed her hand and held out to her his half-smoked Marlboro; she took it and went back to her chair, where she tried to settle. 'It's true, we're not romantic in fiction, and we're even less romantic in real life. Men come and go, they fuck us over, impregnate the hell out of us, project their fantasies onto us and then disappear in a flash. It doesn't leave much room for romance – unless, of course, that's your definition of romance.' Dean went over to the whitewashed wall, leaned against it and slid slowly down to his heels like a man shot in a movie. 'Do you think I'm exaggerating?'

'Did I say you were?' With his head tipped back against the brick, he crouched with his eyes closed, grinning.

'You implied with a certain wrinkling of your forehead that I might be overstating the case. A thing you do with your eyebrows.'

'If that's how you see it, Laura, how can it be an exaggeration?'

'Oh, Dean.' She dropped the dead butt into a pot of wasted fern and wiped her hot hands on the skirt of her dress. 'You're so brilliant – you should have been a lawyer or an astronaut or something.' In the living room the midi system played a driving tunes freebee CD from a Sunday paper, and in that moment it began to skip... *Hotel... Hotel... Hotel California*.

'I *should* have been an astronaut – I would have liked that.'

Laura frowned; she'd never quite fallen in love with his flippancy, which she knew was odd in that he was flippant most of the time, and so indeed was she. 'Men just like to think they're romantic because it gives them something to do in a relationship. Otherwise, they'd be unemployed.'

'Conversely,' he began, and then stopped as a cloud of smoke burst around his head – he'd forgotten to exhale. He stood and came across the tiny garden to take his place on the second chair. From over the wall they heard the commentator exclaim and a round of clapping, cut short as the neighbour turned off the TV.

'Conversely?'

'Conversely, women want men to be devoted to them, like God or their father or a male concubine, then provide for every aspect of their material life.

102

They want a breadwinner who wins bread all day and reads them bedtime stories at night before screwing them senseless.' There was a momentary gap in the evening air, a sweet hiatus not filled by the sound of cars or planes. 'They want a daddy who knows it all and a businessman who writes poetry. They want the lot.'

'That sounds really hard.'

'It's a lifetime's work for a fucking Superman.'

'Tell me honestly, Dean, have you ever actually tried to be Superman?'

He sat with his head bowed, all colour gone from his face, like Chatterton dying in a heatwave. Little rivers of sweat ran from his temples; she felt cool by contrast, in her light dress and minimal lingerie. 'Oh Laura,' he said, 'let's not do gender politics, it's just too hot.' He shut his eyes and shuddered, as if shivering in the heat. Was he about to pass out, she wondered, before she could make a pass?

'For what is it too hot?' She looked around for something to revive him, but saw nothing to hand on her patio.

'Too hot for talking or drinking or sex.'

'We've done two of those three things already, Dean, in our time. How about I make us a jug of Margarita, how does that sound?'

He opened his eyes and blinked. 'It sounds too good to be true. You really have all the ingredients?'

'I knew you were coming round.'

Back in the kitchen, she felt his eyes on her hands as she sliced the limes, set the jug and glasses on a tray, salted the rims and licked her fingers. 'You could have been a cocktail waitress,' he said, after a while, 'somewhere upscale.'

'Do you even know what I do for a living?' She lifted the tray to carry it out, but Dean shook his head.

'Let's stay in here, it's cooler in the kitchen.' They sat and faced one another across the large rectangle of white beech. 'I know you like to draw stuff,' he said, visibly lolling for his drink.

'Bingo.' She poured their Margaritas and lifted her glass in a silent toast. 'So what kind of *stuff* do I like to draw?'

'Oh, I don't know.' Taking a long cool slug, he held the glass against his forehead and closed his eyes for long enough that she began to suspect he was actually asleep. When he opened them again, he looked startled to find her there, staring back into his own bruised stare. 'I've seen you doodling on napkins in restaurants. I guess you have a gift.'

'I'm an architect, Dean, as well you know. I draw bathrooms and kitchens. I drew this one when we moved in.' She smiled as he pressed the glass to his forehead again. 'But we're not defined by our jobs, I hope.'

'I would certainly hope not.'

'But you think, huh, an architect, how unromantic – how tediously pragmatic and in a way cunning. People will always want to redesign their lofts. Old Laura's fixed for life.'

Dean rolled his eyes. 'Of course, there are romantic women, but they're usually bonkers. You see them out jogging with headphones on, trying to sublimate their urges, or doing lengths at the pool, trying to drown some hopeless crush in chlorine.'

She took a deep breath and tried to count backwards to ten – she knew there was no point in losing her temper with him – but there wasn't enough oxygen in the air for it to calm her. 'Is that it then, Dean? Am I just not crazy enough for you? Do I not swim enough lengths in the cause of romantic love?' She set her glass down on the table between them with a click; the midi system had fallen silent on the dying fall of *More Than A Feeling*. Dean simply shrugged, laughed and took another slug of his drink, as if he genuinely didn't understand what she was flying off the handle about. 'So go on – tell me who does it for you, Dean.'

As the sun sank below the rooftops, she listened to Dean lay out her rival in novelistic detail. He described his first visit to her sordid flat, talked about her warped psyche and sullen nature, hinted blandly at her prowess between the sheets. In the sinking glow, his story seemed to hold him spellbound; his deathmask lifted and his eyes began to gleam – he seemed almost to levitate, inspired to a kind of poetry by his lady of the golden mouth.

During this recital of the other woman's quirks and virtues, Laura drank half a jug of Margarita. When he'd finished, she looked on him anew. 'So that's who you're with, when you're not with me.'

'Most of the time.'

'I thought she must be very beautiful and very clever,' Laura went on, 'Marie Curie and Grace Kelly rolled into one.'

Dean laughed shortly. 'Well, I can see why you might want to think that way.' He put his elbows on the table, cradling his cold glass. The night outside suggested an urban maelstrom, as if responding to Dean's story with sirens, caterwauls and screeching tyres, which zoomed through the whorled heat and barged into the kitchen. 'But really, Laura, it's not as if you and I were an item.'

A fine fury descended on her then, like a feather from the ceiling. She shook her head slowly from side to side, gripping the edge of her beautiful table as if in pain. 'I know you think I'm a snob, Dean. But Jesus Christ – a dumb Polack!'

'Your racism is not your most endearing quality, Laura. She comes from Moldova, a small country to the east of Romania. And for your information she's far from dumb.'

'Oh my God, Dean, I know where Moldova is.' She seized the jug, tilting it so violently that icecubes flew across the tiles. 'Everything you say about her screams DUMB, from her crappy job to her crappy lifestyle.' She slammed the jug down and thrust her face in his. 'I know what you're like, Dean. You think it's funny to fuck an imbecile. You think you've made some kind of morganatic marriage to the farmer's daughter, like you're the dauphin and she's the whore.'

Dean grinned shakily, clearly wanting to make light of their quarrel. 'Okay, so she didn't go to college, Laura. But at the end of the day she's worth a dozen of us, for all our quips and gambits and witty encapsulations.'

Laura put her face in her hands and tried to breathe; the night had again fallen almost silent, as if awaiting the outcome of this exchange. A few doors down, her neighbour jacked up his stereo and the opening chords of *Big Calm* came through the french windows, spreading its chill, as if he'd been looking for and finally found an appropriate soundtrack for this scene. She took her hands from her face. 'And have you told her about us?'

'Have I told her *what* about us?' Dean sighed as if weary of her questions and qualms. 'Monika doesn't get off on stuff like that – she isn't decadent the way we are. I mean, she went to church every Sunday when she was a kid. She found the man she wanted to stay with for the rest of her life, then he left her and she lost her faith. It's like she broke up with God just to go out with me.'

Laura stood abruptly and fetched what was left of the Vermouth, gathering a bottle of bourbon from the sideboard in the living room. Back in the kitchen, she grabbed the empty jug from the table and flung the remaining ice into the sink. She felt his eyes on her as she marched around the room.

'What are you doing?'

'I'm making Manhattans, to remind me of my wedding day.'

'Of course,' he said, 'we keep forgetting that you're married.'

'Don't patronise me, Russler.' She grabbed his Margarita from his hand and threw the contents through the door into the garden. When a minute later she set down before him a tumbler full of

Vermouth and whiskey, he leaned back in his seat, his pale face a picture of complacency. He went on smoking and drinking as if nothing had transpired, while she quivered in her seat. She felt less focused, less eloquent and more defeated with her first sip of her fresh drink. 'You enjoy this kind of shit though, don't you Dean? It's like you really dig other people's pain.'

'No, Laura. I dig their complexity. You see the difference?'

Perspiring in her alligator dress, muddled by the conflicting alcohols and worn out by this argument in a moral vacuum, it struck her that Alberto was out there wandering London alone, driven from his home by her cavalier guest. She hated to think of her husband as lonely or wretched – she still loved him in her way, even if she was fondest in his absence, when there was no immediate prospect of his return. A tenet she clung to, a principle she held onto firmly was that people belonged to one another forever, no matter how often they stabbed each other in the back or abandoned each other in moments of crisis. Everyone she knew was free to paddle in her great pool of love; anyone who liked could wade in from the bank, no one was excluded – or almost no one. She was not about to share it with some overgrown nymphet.

Dean sat across from her in his damp shirt, totally unperturbed. Okay, perhaps he was a teensy bit disappointed by the turn their talk had taken, but that was all. Oh, Dean was so serene! It was part of his appeal, of course, but tonight she wished that something would come along and shatter his complacency. She wished his life would finally break him, so he'd crawl back to her with his ego snapped in two, a changed man.

'Look,' he said, 'let's get this straight. I only told you about Monika because I thought it would tickle you – and because you have a right to know who I'm fucking, as a friend.'

'Let's get this even straighter, Dean. You are weak, weak, weak. You want *me* to be as weak as *you* are, so we can skulk around feeling low and sick about the rotten way we live. You know the way we live is trash, Dean, and that girl is the trashiest thing yet.'

Finally provoked by this insult to his paramour, he stood and walked to the kitchen door, where his jacket hung from a hook. She scrambled to her feet. 'I haven't finished with you yet,' she yelled – then she fell in a heap at his feet, watching herself fall, seeing herself for a second like Madame Butterfly or La Dame aux Camélias, enfeebled by cocktails and the long fiasco of her seduction. Dean left his jacket and helped her up, and she sat again and wept into her Manhattan, sensing his bewilderment in the face of her tears.

'I didn't mean to hurt you, honey,' she heard him say; he'd taken his seat across from her again. 'You're still my cherry pie,' he murmured. 'My cherry pie with all the cherries missing.'

At this she raised her head and grabbed his wrist, yanking down so hard that he was dragged across the table. 'You want to see how fucking crazy I can get? Is that it, Dean?' It must have looked to him as if she was about kiss his palm – but instead she sank her teeth into the flesh at the base of his thumb. He struggled at the end of her incisors until she released him, and then he sprang up and jumped around the kitchen, clutching his hand and dripping blood across the tiles. For a minute or more there was only the sound of his groans, the chirruping of a car alarm and wafts of Morcheeba. Laura wiped his blood from her lips, tasting him on her tongue – and he crossed the floor at last and pulled her to her feet, smearing the waist of her favourite dress as he kissed her on the mouth.

So they stood there for some time, exchanging blood and spit and tears, Laura drinking in her success. But even as he held her in his arms she felt a misgiving, wondered whether it wouldn't have been best to turn him out of the house as soon as he mentioned the other woman. He'd shown her where she stood and then she'd pushed him till he cracked – but that had been the moment to release him, maybe. She should have let him go back to his games and books and scenes, to carrying his satchel from station to station – she wouldn't even have to wonder how it ended. He'd do the same thing over and over with diminishing virility until he drifted into some backwater, where old men's bones would thrill to his tales of ill-gotten bliss.

But now that she'd got him to cross the floor to her at last, she couldn't let him go. She let his kisses wind her up until she must have him inside her or implode, until she ran upstairs with him to her marital bed and unzipped his dirty fly. The first time it was quickly over – for a few minutes they lay back, glassy-eyed and gasping – but then they came together again with the same warlike urgency. It was true that with him inside her she could read his thoughts. *Here we go*, she heard him thinking, *two carnal heroes of the underground, adding another chapter, making it up as we go along*. She could read his thoughts, but even in the midst of their flailing around his feelings remained perfectly opaque. But she could have all these thoughts herself and still fuck – she was subtle enough to fuck and think –

and even while she wondered *who* he was, *where* he was and *how* he could still hide at a moment like this, she thought this might be her only time with Dean Russler. So she made the most of it – too much, in fact, until the sex lost any suggestion of tenderness. But that night at least, spurred on no doubt by adrenaline and alcohol and the novelty of his cock in her cunt, he was everything she'd hoped he would be.

Until dawn she lay trapped in a cycle of fucking, sleeping, waking and fucking. But she must have finally fallen asleep, because she woke to the din of birds in the trees on the street, hearing the key turn in the lock downstairs. She leaned up on an elbow and looked down on Dean, whose face was grey in the morning light, his breathing shallow; a scab had formed around his thumb. Hearing footsteps on the stairs, she thought maybe she should wake him, but her thinking was no more organised than the rooftop chorus – a bluebird of happiness battling it out with a blackbird of doom. Her limbs were so liquidised by sex that she could only wait where she was, holding her breath against the moment of discovery.

The dull clump of her husband's tread came to an end at the head of the stairs. She heard him sigh before he walked across the landing to the open door – she awaited the instant when he would stand in the doorway and see them lying together, one awake and one comatose, each sticky with the other's juices. And when he appeared, framed by the rectangle of pine, she would see him in all his dignity, like the portrait of an artist in the age of Vasari – on the run from the Pope, but with his pride still intact. This was what she was waiting to see. But when Alberto at last appeared in the doorway, he showed neither pain nor surprise; he had that look on his face that he sometimes wore when she forgot to put out the bins. He stared at her, gave her half a minute of unblinking resentment, then clumped off to sleep on the zed-bed she kept in her studio. And that was it, his cuckold's revenge – that was his version of a vendetta.

## Satori on the Heath

The summer did its usual thing: blossomed, became overly intense in scattered moments then dwindled, leaving a sense that although in theory there were several weeks of the season left, in fact it was nearly done. On the last day of July, a Saturday, Dean was due to take Monika out into the country. His plan was to catch a train to a rural location, buy a room beside a river and watch sunlight fall through hotel curtains. And she'd agreed to this, albeit with no great eagerness. It would be good for her, he insisted; she was hypertense, so citified that she was almost part of the street furniture – lost in a fog, even if it was a fog of her own making. He made these observations to himself, merely saying to her that the hot July had been hard on her system and she needed to chill. While she only shrugged and rolled her eyes and lit another spliff, she seemed to accept the need for chilling.

The arrangement had been made at the last minute, on Thursday night – then over the phone on Saturday morning she'd called it off, telling him in her lifeless stoner tones that she was needed at work. This was at least plausible; she did work Saturdays now and then, though only when she volunteered for a shift. So his weekend all at once had nothing in it, with his weekend lover suddenly unavailable, and on Saturday lunchtime, instead of sitting on a train with her as he'd envisaged and heading for Whitstable or Didcot or wherever they might have gone, he found himself wandering from his flat to Camden Lock, as he did every other Saturday, in search of a secondhand book.

He scanned the stacks, expecting the weather to turn, watching the clouds for rain and glancing at his watch, trying to settle with his higher power on a good moment to start the day's drinking. He could drink, or he could go home and write to Estelle, who he barely remembered, whose address he'd lost; those were the options. Looking up from the hands again, both of them stuck at midday, he saw his waitress approach over the bridge that straddled the canal, between two willow trees. She couldn't be coming to see *him*, of course – but here she was, up in Camden, only a few hours after blowing him off on the pretext of work. She was on the upper level, he on the lower; from afar, he saw her hover at a stall full of trendy trifles and New Age frippery, and in a reflex he turned back to the book stacks.

Every weekend pretty much he bought an old paperback and read it till it died. He read it on the Underground on his way to work, during lunch and over dinner, in the bath and on the toilet, until all the pages fell out – so it was only natural that in this crisis he should bury himself in a book. Flicking through a decrepit Penguin edition of *Enemies of Promise*, he lost himself in it for a minute or two – but when he looked up to see Monika emerge from a tie-die emporium and walk in her slinky way back towards the water, he shoved the book in the rack and began to run after her in pursuit.

He began, but then he stopped. What was he doing, where was his head? Laura was the one he should be pursuing, not this waitress with her tunnel vision, her mindless beauty. He imagined bumping into Laura in the market, how he'd tap her on the shoulder and how she'd turn and look him over with that sardonic glimmer in her eye. 'Did you know that casual sex is one of the enemies of promise?' he'd ask. 'And you, Dean, are the enemy of promises,' she'd reply – and they'd roll around laughing and go to a bar, order themselves a Martini and talk about everything and nothing till it was time to fake another orgasm. Why was he chasing Monika when he could be lying in bed with Laura, who was so constant, or anyway consistent, whose friendship was like one long conversation?

'Call her, call her and let the other one be,' he told himself, in the wake of his vanishing Moldovan. But even as he said it he started to run again after the one who had no real interest in him, who barely saw him at all.

He caught up with her just as she reached the tables beneath the nearest willow tree by the canal. She stood perching on the sides of her feet, as she sometimes did in absent moments, studying the specials board outside the café. He put out a hand to touch her back and she felt the contact and swung around, flinging out her arms as if to defend herself, opening her mouth as if to scream. When she saw that it was only Dean, not the immigration geek or her long-lost fiancé or one of her druggy demons made flesh – oh, the look she gave him! It was as if he'd torn off a mask to reveal her true face, carved from alabaster and with emeralds for eyes. She was stoned, of course, which may have been why she looked at him so stonily, but her reaction froze his tongue at the very moment when he needed to say something, something clownish and idiotic, the kind of thing that made her giggle when they were horizontal and she was out of her tree. He needed to persuade her that he hadn't followed her all the way from Streatham Hill to Camden; he knew that was how it looked. But for a crucial moment he was lost for words, while his gaze travelled of its own accord from her green eyes to the hollow of her throat – and the sky turned leaden, as if filled with zeppelins.

With a shake of her shoulders she shook herself free of his hand, and he reeled back a step, stumbling on the cobbles while she stood off from him and tugged at her bra-strap through the cotton of her top. She gave him the same frown she'd given him that first time they'd met, in the casino; the corners of her mouth turned down so far that her dimples seemed to pop. 'Oh, fuck it,' he thought, stepping forward to kiss her. Surely he could kiss her, at least; after all, they still hooked up almost every time they met, even if the frequency of those encounters was decreasing. But the kiss did not come off – she averted her face with a sigh – and in that moment he found himself hating this cold fish, this peasant who took him for a cop and spurned him in the marketplace.

He might have made some cutting remark and walked away, but in the awkward seconds that followed a man materialised from inside the café and greeted her familiarly, as if they'd known each other for a while. He was tall and young, younger and taller than Dean and coated in black leather, with wet-look gel in his hair. But no – the look was natural; it had started to rain. A sudden summer deluge fell on the falafels and sweatshirts and homemade jewellery, bootleg tapes and jerk chicken, postcards of old punks and the books in the bookstalls. As the stallholders emerged with sheets of plastic to cover their goods, Dean watched the leather man put an arm around his waitress and lead her away through the crowd that flowed over the bridge. She disappeared into the blurry scene, the grey background, and he turned and walked in the other direction, towards Hampstead Heath.

The weather had been threatening to turn since breakfast, but still it caught him unawares in his brown suede jacket, lumberjack shirt and chinos. He walked on into the deluge in a trance of anguish, splashing along the pavement in his holey Docs, trouser-legs molded to his thighs and hair plastered to his scalp, chanting wordlessly as he went. For a mile or so, he was unaware of his surroundings; he only saw where he was when, totally soaked, he found himself climbing the rainswept sward of Parliament Hill. 'Oh this, and that, and this,' he chuntered, to prevent himself from saying anything more coherent. 'Yeah, you do the watusi, you do the watusi,' he wittered, as he sat for a mad moment on a bench with the wildest, wettest view back over the city – the brutal, stupid city.

Blindly he meandered across the Heath until he came to the bathing pools, where water dashed into water and sent up tiny clear spirals. On the bank of the first pool stood the narrow figure of a man whose shape and features were blurred in the downpour, an impression made flesh – he might have been anything between 17 or 70. He stood poised with his toes on the edge, made an arc and broke the surface, which closed over him with extraordinary finality. Dean stood under the huge, broken umbrella of an oak and watched for a watery eternity until the man resurfaced; he seemed not to realise that he'd been away from the world for so long – he swam to the side, clambered out and dived again. A lifetime went by between each dive, a lifetime in which Dean envied the diver his oneness with the wetness. Oh, how he would have liked to fling off his sodden clothes, run howling into the pool and dissolve – let his ego fall apart and let the pieces sink to the muddy bottom. Oh, to dissolve!

But the water would be cold, and the world seemed a cold enough place already. He wandered away from the ponds and stopped in a copse of beeches, under a mature tree massive enough to provide shelter. The tree seemed oddly familiar, as if it was someone he knew, or had known, and he lifted his face and yelled at the top of his voice into its upper branches, a yell that turned into a wail. And why not wail? There was no one to hear him, after all, or nothing but the tree.

'I have no career, no wife,' he declared, 'I have no idea how to get a career or a wife.' He looked up to see how the tree was taking his confession, and a little bucket of rain fell from the upper branches into his face, dousing him. 'I have none of the things people like me are supposed to have – I have no focus or raison d'être, no depth or substance, my achievements could be listed on a blade of grass.' He paused, as if this ancient presence might somehow respond. 'Do you think that is very bad?'

The tree made no comment, and Dean left its sanctuary and went back into the rain. He walked on over the Heath beneath a sky that seemed to go on getting closer, a sinking ceiling without angels or a chink of light. He aimed his waterlogged steps towards the shiny prosperity of Hampstead and its beautiful pubs, knowing that from inside The Flask, even if its snugness was akin to smugness, even if its cosiness was ersatz, the sky would return to its usual scale. Out here on the Heath, in this summer that was no longer a summer, he was exposed to the opinions of Nature, in whose eyes he was not even a no one. But in The Flask, with a pint of Youngs before him on the table, like a madman taking his first sip of poison, for a while he could escape the knowledge that he was alone in the world, and that unrequited lust was just a little tedious.

But oh, what a waste. Here he was, Dean Russler, fool for love, when once he might have been something quite different – a bingo caller or a compere in a variety club. He might have learned how to play bridge like Omar Sharif, or edited a dictionary on Alphabet Street, looked out for the puffins on Puffin Island. He might have been a spy, a dean, a gigolo, the oldest bellboy at the Ritz, the Bohemian ambassador or the court pornographer. Emerging from his watery wilderness at last onto the high street, he was almost knocked sideways by the weight of the wind and his regrets. How had he fallen so thoroughly for the plan, when he could have been a pleasure boat captain – when there might have been some other way to be?

## Laura's Dilemma II

Laura could have dreamed up a more evil scenario than the present, and so she consoled herself. Alberto and Dean would come to bed and make love to her, and at times it felt like a feast, on those days when she had Alberto for breakfast and Dean for lunch, evenings when she had the pick of them – but there were nights when neither turned up for dinner, and she was caught between cravings. Of course, neither was bound to her in any real sense: Alberto was only in name her husband, and with Dean it was clear that she was second best. Then it frustrated her that they took so little notice of each other. Since the night of the bitten thumb, she'd slept with Dean in her marital bed with little consciousness of doing wrong, since Alberto kept such a low profile. She explained away his absences, ascribing to him some wicked pursuit. 'He's away seeing his mistress in Golders Green, he's off playing poker all night with the bakery guys, he's doing coke in the West End with his City buddies.' But she knew that Dean gave no credence to the alibis she invented for his rival and had no curiosity about his whereabouts.

She told herself that she had what she wanted – two men on a plate of sorts – but it came at a cost. Alternately loved up and neglected, burned out by the dual stimuli of husband and lover or left entirely alone, for days in a row she wandered the house in a robe, slack and listless and applying herself to nothing. During those long afternoons she'd look to the future and tell herself that Dean was merely a forerunner, the real thing was still to come. And it was true that as a lover he was a disappointment, not as she'd imagined. After that first night of carnal intensity, their lovemaking had quickly become formulaic.

'But how can it be anything else?' Dean asked her, one evening when she brought it up. 'We have sex the way old friends have sex.'

'It's a funny kind of friendship,' she replied, 'when we know almost nothing about each other.'

Dean leaned up on his elbow and traced a line around her nipple through her tiny blonde hairs. 'If there was anything important you needed to know about me, you would have worked it out by now. You have this second sight or fifth sense or something. It's one of the things I love about you.'

In a way he was right, of course. Simply from listening in and reading between the lines she knew his daily routine, his morning glory and evening taper. She knew that before he went out at night he'd dance to the Stones with one hand waving free and the other clutching a bottle of Pinot Grigio, that he still beat himself up over his second class degree, preferred blueberries to blackberries and raspberries to strawberries, that he hankered after simplicity even while he added another strand to his tangled web. She knew that his worst nightmare was to wake up and find that a dog had eaten his nose – and how he loved to drink himself into a stupor at least twice a week, and how he expected to spend the rest of his life this way. She intuited his peculiar fetishes and weird private trips – but surely intimacy was made of more than just hunches. She wanted him to lay himself bare, to show her that she in some way possessed him.

'So you want full disclosure?' said Dean. 'I'm not a full disclosure kind of guy.' He sat up in bed – in her conjugal bed again, one afternoon – and took a sip from his frosty alcopop. 'I leave that kind of stuff to other people, Laurie.'

'So why do you keep a diary? You must tell secrets to that notebook that you don't tell me.'

'There are no secrets in my diary,' he told her. 'It's just a record of events, in my uneventful life. It simply describes what anyone can see on the surface.' She was sure he was lying, but what could she say? 'There are things I'd never tell anyone,' he held up to the light his bottle of saccharine fizz, 'however long I lived.'

'While I preach openness to the rest of the world, I remain the human clam myself,' she mocked, mimicking his voice.

'I don't say them,' he said, 'and I don't even think them.'

Laura leaned back against the headboard and closed her eyes. 'You must whisper them in your heart though, I guess.'

And then they made love – but she felt no closer to him during it or afterwards, and she sensed that to him it didn't matter.

She sought stratagems to make him care, tried to build in his head an image of herself that he could take home, a snapshot to keep by his bedside. Like any man, he responded to certain signals; she had only to break his code, she thought, to make him fully hers. She teased out his predilections and fed her findings to him one by one, noting that he liked to hear of her youthful frustrations and adolescent lusts and her later moments of fecklessness, such as the night in New York when she paid a bouncer for sex. He lapped up her stories – but she knew that even so her attractions were limited, that to Dean she was just a roll in the hay, and a quick one at that. He liked round figures, and she was all bones; he liked feeble-minded geese, not intellectual hawks. Once he jokingly compared her to a lizard, and afterwards it came to her that he didn't even really like the way she kissed. But still she went on trying to find the key.

'When I was 16,' she told him one afternoon, as they sat on their bench on Clapham Common, 'I was so chubby that when I ran for the school bus my bra-strap snapped in two.'

Dean laughed. 'That's good,' he nodded. She looked at him, remembering the first time they'd walked on the Common together, around the pond in late spring, when seeds like silver parachutes fell around them in the bright air.

'Then there was the afternoon when I found out about my piano.'

'Your piano?'

'I played it from the age of eight – very badly, of course. Then one day I stood up to change the music and I felt the keyboard press against me, right here.' She took his hand and pressed it between her legs; an old man walking his dog stopped dead in his tracks, shook his head and walked on. 'I rubbed up against the middle C. It was a lot more fun than practising scales, I can tell you.'

'That's so cute,' said Dean, retrieving his hand and lighting another cigarette. 'I shall always think of you as the young pianist, playing arpeggios with her clitoris.' He took the hipflask from his pocket and unscrewed the cap. The remnants of his fringe – his hairline seemed to recede daily – shone with south London light. She would have liked to know him with a full head of hair. 'But you must have had your Tess of the d'Urbervilles moment. You're a country girl, right? You grew up in the country.'

Laura looked down at her naked toes, poking from her sandals; she liked them – they were long and elegant, like the rest of her, but useful too. They stopped her from falling on her face.

'The country has lost something since the days of Thomas Hardy. I mean, no one ever tried to fuck me in a ditch. In the end,' she sighed, 'I lost my hymen to a horse.' Dean sat with his elbows resting on the back of the bench, blowing smoke into the warm, still air of late summer. Above them was a blue immensity, too pure to be alluring. Laura reached over and borrowed his lighter. 'Not much fun at the time, but sweet in the memory. He was a nice little pony. Do you find this at all interesting, Dean?'

He turned to her with a look of surprise. 'But of course I do. You know I hang on your every word.' When she laughed he said, 'But I really do. I wish I could travel back to your past, watch you ride bareback across the fields again.'

'My parents still live there. It's wonderful, but I don't go home as often as I should.' She smiled across at him. 'It's one of those places you visit meaning to stay for a couple of days and you end up staying a month. I'm always afraid I'll get stuck and never leave.' Even as she spoke she saw his eyes lose focus, his attention shift inwards or away.

'What about your parents? You never talk about them, or not to me.'

'They're dead,' he said, firing his butt at a scruffy pigeon. 'Sad, isn't it? Tragic, really. But at least their bodies are safe from body snatchers, sealed up in the Russler mausoleum in Nunhead Cemetery with only squirrels for company.'

'God, Dean, I'm sorry. I never knew.' Rocked by this information, Laura lit a Sobranie and watched him take a series of quick nips from his hipflask. There was a point in the afternoon when whatever he kept in there began to affect him, his speech became richer and less precise and his eyes slid away into pathless interzones. It was happening to him now, she realised; she'd lose him soon. 'But that explains so much. I mean, no wonder you're so...'

He looked at her sharply from the corner of his eye. 'So what?'

'Oh, I don't know. Adrift, rootless, rudderless. That kind of thing.'

Dean gazed at her steadily. 'I was only kidding, Laura. They're not dead, or not in the way you're thinking. They have not literally ceased to be. They're alive and well and living in Dulwich. I just think of them as being dead because it feels more natural. I get a sense of closure, you know.'

'Jesus, Dean.' She stood abruptly and threw her slender cigarette into the early evening breeze. Walking to the edge of the pond she stood, looking over the shoulder of a fisherman. They'd missed him there, among the reeds; he must have heard every word. Her eyes watered, her belly sang with need; she wanted to wander out into the middle of the little concrete pond and lie down among the lilies like Ophelia. She wanted to be as unlike Dean's parents as possible – either utterly alive or utterly dead.

He came and stood by her side. 'I'd better be off,' was his only comment. 'Gathering moss and all that.'

'You could come back for dinner.' She remained where she was, her back to him. 'It would be just you and me and the mystery cat.' She looked down at the slimy waters of the stagnant pool, at the back of the fisherman's head. 'You know which mystery cat I mean.' It was one of those vacant midweek evenings at the height of summer, when solitude, even for the psychologically sturdy, is hard to bear. She turned to face him; his eyes were fixed on the ground between their feet. 'Alberto's not around.'

'Why, have you locked him in the cellar again?'

'He's away at a conference in Strasbourg, a meeting of minds. I think he took his fancy woman.'

She rubbed her long nose. 'We won't be seeing him for a while, at any rate.'

'Splendid. Well, don't you get too lonely now.' Dean began to walk away. She followed him at the distance of a yard or two, wanting to wring his neck. It was humiliating to have so little control over a man who was so weak-willed. But he strode out ahead and she had to run to catch up with him – which she did, outside the gaping concrete maw of Clapham South tube station, waylaying him with a hand on his arm. 'What about tomorrow night?'

'Maybe, sweetheart.' He seemed to soften when he saw the tears in her eyes. 'We'll get together again soon.'

'Are you going home now, Dean?'

'I don't think so, no.'

'You're going to look for her.' To this he made no answer, and she changed tack. 'Do you like what we have, Dean? Does it make you happy?'

'Of course.' He reached out and touched the curve of her cheek. 'I've never been friends with a woman before.'

'And you like our friendship just the way it is.'

'Yes,' he said. 'I do.' He looked over her shoulder to the entrance of the station. It was rush hour; hundreds of suited and booted men and women poured forth from the Underground. The blue light in the sky began to fade. 'It has a precious quality all its own,' he said. 'A je ne sais quoi. A quiet genius.'

And then he turned and left, as she knew he would, leaving her to sing *Ne Me Quitte Pas*, to bring some formality and dignity to her feelings of rejection. Where he went and what he did were his own business; she could find no way to change that, no lure or means of entrapment. But still she couldn't quite bring herself to let him go.

# The Neverending Search

The weekend of his Satori marked the start of what Dean called in his diary **The Neverending Search**. It began right there, the moment when Monika's back was turned, when he walked out of Camden Lock market and took his turn in the rain.

At the next opportunity he asked for her mobile number, a move he'd resisted up to now, since having her number meant in his mind some crude elimination of obstacles, taking a short cut through space and time. He had no faith in short cuts. But his credit card company had given him a mobile, a burgundy brick with a black antenna – and now he was reduced to calling his waitress at all hours, only to find that her phone was switched off, or he got through but her hushed tones were drowned out by other sounds. When he asked her where she was exactly, the line – although there was no line, only satellites – would go weird and crackly, and he could hear only the distorted racket behind her, salsa music in a club perhaps or some cheesy porn soundtrack or the Union Jack guitar shit that people still went for that summer. The backing track was never the same, but she always claimed to be at home or at work, insisted in her careless whisper that she was putting in the hours at the casino or sleeping off the effects. And he knew, in his heart of hearts, that neither of those things were true.

However slim the prospect of tracking her down, he couldn't help going out to look, stepping from doorways into the rain, too antsy to wait for the rain to stop. Throughout August he walked down soulless boulevards, anonymous avenues peopled by grotesques – those same citizens he'd looked on with such sentimental warmth at the height of summer when they were witnesses to his trysts with her and, once or twice, the act of love itself. He recalled the evening on Frith Street when he'd fucked her with his fingers while the crowd rushed by. Reflected in their spectacles through a blue filter of midsummer sky, he and she had shone like fallen stars in some dirty romance. But as summer fell into a succession of wet days broken up by an occasional day of mad heat, when steam rose from gutters and people had to shed a skin to survive, his onetime audience looked as miserable as he felt – drifting down the street as if floating along the River Styx with pennies on their eyes, a hint of what awaited him if he failed to find his Moldovan.

He acknowledged that his pursuit of this green-eyed minx across the London labyrinth had the status of myth, and at times he could almost convince himself that it was mostly the myth that he loved. Perhaps the tale of a sad scribe pursuing his Slavonic pixie across the boulevards of the metropolis was a literary creation more than anything else, and one he'd contrived from the start. This was a comforting notion, even if it took nothing away from the pain he felt in her absence. Yet surely even the pain was contrived: in devoting himself to someone so mercurial, wasn't he just exercising his masochistic tendencies? Like any other middleclass boy brought up in the soft embrace of secular capitalism, he liked to be brutalised now and then to know he was alive – to have a pretty lady squeeze his balls. He could tell himself this; but then the agony returned, as if Monika had discovered the masochist's Achilles heel, so great that it wiped out all pleasure.

Monika had a routine of no routine, and Dean could never be sure at what hour of day or night she might turn up – but since she'd never reclaimed her key, he could always let himself into her flat. He'd make a drink, roll himself a joint and then, sitting in an armchair with sunken springs in the awful wasteland of her lounge, eyed by the tiger on the wall, he'd read his novel and wait on her return. If it was his lucky night he'd hear her key turn in the lock after midnight, hear her slingbacks fall from her feet in the hallway, the earphones of her CD Walkman playing out some dreadful ditty by Dido or Alanis Morissette. She'd come in without even a glance in his direction, slump on the sofa and roll a spliff, light it with her Zippo, lean back and inhale. As the drug slipped into her bloodstream she might begin to register his presence, shooting a look at his face as if he were no more than a funny hallucination.

But he wasn't always alone. On many occasions when he turned up at her flat, he could rely on her landlord to welcome him with a shot of vodka and a mournful smile. Humberto was Colombian, in his mid-forties, pockmarked and genial and never out of his tracksuit bottoms. He sublet to Monika at mate's rates, although she wasn't really a mate – he was just a soft touch, as he said himself – her meagre rent adding to his shitty hospital porter pay. He had no social life to speak of, but this was no reflection on his personality; he was just too poor and clever to join the clubs that would have him or form his own cliques. Dean understood his dilemma, in that he also lacked people he could call up and chat to. In truth he'd never been that stuck on conversing with men – they meant little to him without their attendant women – but Humberto was a sweet guy, without face or side; for him he could make an exception.

So Humberto would hang out with him on the countless evenings when he failed to find his stoner girl at home, and they'd get in beers and a takeaway and talk about their lives. Dean found nothing much to say about his 32 years; what was most important to him at that moment – his black star, on which no words could shed light – was already known to Humberto. But over a can of Red Stripe and a kebab, the Colombian spoke of his teaching career in Bogotá, the woman he'd had married for the wrong reasons and the kid he'd left behind. One night he fished out from between the sofa cushions a dusty pink vibrator, the same that Dean had seen that first night. 'She leaves it lying around,' the landlord said, 'Sometimes when she gets drunk she pretends it's a microphone and sings into it. Really, that girl is so childish.'

If Humberto was at work, he'd go to her room in the hope of finding her between the sheets, cowering from her dope visions, as now and then he still did. But more often than not he'd turn on her bedside lamp and find her bed empty and unmade. It was always dusk when he arrived; outside the day would always be declining, all along her road streetlights flickering on, casting luminous orange against a grainy grey sky. He'd take off his shoes and make himself a joint from the doings in her top drawer then lie back and smoke it, watching himself in the ceiling mirror. In the dim light and cracked silver he saw a man almost at ease in the world – stoned and raggedy in his frayed shirt, but the closest he could come to happiness. After all, there was an odd kind of relief in knowing she was elsewhere, and he need look no further that night.

Lying on her bed without her, he'd think about her sad girl act, her exile from everything, her sexual monism. At first he'd supposed that she smoked mainly to numb the pain of being abandoned in the giant void where her man had left her – and that was surely part of it, although the drug sometimes had the opposite effect. Sometimes it opened a door to her sadness, set her off on crying jags that nothing could interrupt, none of his jokes or kisses, leaving her like a damp rag at the end of an hour. But those collapses were outnumbered by times when smoking simply shut her down, closed down all her centres except the one that was easiest to satisfy, her libido. Then she became impossible to reach through speech, as if she'd found some way of totally absenting herself and leaving just her nerve endings, membranes and reflexes. If her habit often cut her off from him, he'd never really egged her to stay straight, because her libido at its utmost was like a miraculous fountain. After a couple of joints, her body would become so sensitised – her ass was one hot zone, her cunt a vessel of liquid heat – that if he touched her anywhere, pulled even lightly on a strand of hair, she reacted with an ardour that looked quite dangerous to the naked eye. But then there were other times when she was neither tearful nor lustful but just fell back in her chair, unable to speak or focus or move more than a finger. 'I'm gone,' was all she'd say, 'I'm gone.'

Measured in calendar days, the neverending search was a brief interlude – but it seemed to last forever, eating up the hours. On Tuesday he closed his eyes in the queue in Sainsbury's, and when he

139

opened them again it was Thursday and his stubble was almost a beard, his broccoli had gone to seed. He tried to put a brake on it, of course – he wasn't actually insane, he reasoned with himself – and some afternoons he hung around at home, listened to *The Bride Stripped Bare* again, or reread *Gatsby*, or tried to write to Estelle. But the words wouldn't come, his head wasn't in it – and who was Estelle again anyway?

One damp evening at the end of August he stood beside the payphones in Victoria station. He'd left his mobile at Laura's the previous night, storming out midway through an alcoholic game of backgammon over some imagined slight – or that was how he wanted it to seem. In fact, the storming out had been for show; he'd only wanted to avoid going to bed with Laura, whose inability to be the other woman, to take on her shape and her scent, depressed him to the nth degree. Now he stood among his hopeless brethren in their raincoats, who held phones in their trembling mitts, shoved coins in the slot and muttered into the receiver, 'Who's there, who is this, is it Mary Lamb, the Pink Floyd, the Samaritans?'

Monika answered once, answered twice, was both times mysteriously cut off – and the whine of disconnection sounded like someone flat-lining after a cardiac arrest, as if her heart had finally died to him and left him a widower. He gripped the handset until his knuckles turned white, and braced himself against the metal column supporting the phone. He could leave all the messages he liked, he could dog her to infinity, but she'd never get back to him.

He lingered by the phones alongside his fellow loiterers and malingerers, who glanced in passing at his pockets, took in his look of shambolic despair and dismissed him as one of their own. Finally, desperate for any conversation, he called Laura on her landline. There was a muffled scrambling at the other end and a period of heavy breathing, and he guessed she'd taken the receiver under the covers with her to shield their chat from Alberto. 'Hi,' he said, closing his eyes and imagining the warmth in there.

'It's just snazzy to hear your voice again, Dean,' she said. 'Say, do you think your parents would have called you Dane if they'd known you'd turn out to be such a hound?'

'I think they thought about it, Laurie Lee. But in the end they called me Dean, after my father.'

'The father you never found.'

'The father I never looked for.'

From under the covers three miles to the south he heard a snuffle and a snort. 'Poor Dean,' she said. 'Were you terribly neglected?'

'I guess some of us were born to suffer and some of us were made to run around like bits of wood till judgment day.' He edged away from his nearest neighbour, who was barking into the receiver a mix of words in no particular order, then hitting it against the pillar between them. The white lettering up on the departures board read CANCELLED CANCELLED CANCELLED, as if no one would ever go anywhere again. 'I'm sorry I ran out on you last night.'

'That's okay,' she said. 'You're in love, you're blind to anyone else's feelings.' She cleared her throat. 'I can hear you're out there, Deano. Go home and get some sleep.'

'I'd like to, Laura, but I don't think I can.'

Ringing off, he walked hurriedly away through the remnants of the grand arch. Victoria station had joined a long list of places that in future he'd need to steer clear of, even if it meant that his journey described a large loop. The capital was dotted with such fatal spots where he'd given in to inescapable truths; one day, in an empty hour, he'd mark them all off in his *A to Z*. He took refuge in The Albert Tavern on Victoria Street – if he had to face up to shit, he preferred to do so on the back of a few pints. The situation was this, he explained to his glass of Carlsberg, using a couple of beermats and a puddle of beer to draw himself a diagram. Monika had been alive to him at the start, perhaps, but her interest in him had quickly waned. His habitual presence kept him in the frame for a while, but by midsummer whatever thrill they had was gone. From that point, he'd simply chosen not to notice his immense irrelevance to her life: she'd continued to tolerate his arrivals and barely registered his departures, getting on with her weird, spacey existence as if they'd never met.

But how could he have let this happen? It was precisely the sort of heartbreak scenario he'd so rigorously avoided since a girl in college put a dent in him in their last term. In the years that followed, he may have felt desolate for a morning now and then, but no one had left him with a wound that didn't heal in a weekend.

He bought another pint, sat down at a different table and watched his thinking circle back around, as it always did on the topic of Monika, so that he ended up facing the point where he'd started. How come she'd picked him up that night, only to drop him again with so little ceremony? Why pluck him from obscurity, only to toss him back? But that was it, he thought – he'd never know. She'd chosen him for a reason born of an impulse conceived in a forest in Transylvania under precious little starlight. But that *was* it, he thought, sitting up straight now with his pint in his hand: she came from a world that still had starlight, where forests and horses and carts, apples and apple farmers weren't just props or pretty details in a novel. She came from another world. How had he never seen it before?

He'd always thought her capriciousness a pose – but what if it was all real, and her fickle nature was not some mask she put on to play the role of femme fatale? She wasn't a faux naive English girl, playing a game she pretended not to understand – she was exactly who she seemed to be. The thought had never entered his mind before, because it was not a quality of anyone else he knew. Everyone else, including him, happily or unhappily played a role; he'd assumed that she was simply doing the same, that her dramatic highs and lows were just part of a performance, put on for his benefit since he was the one in the room. What if she was just being herself?

He finished his pint and ran back to the payphones in the station, where the long whine of disconnection was replaced by a voice that said, 'Please replace the handset and try again... please replace the handset and try again... please replace the handset...' The toneless voice had put him off before – but this time the robot was right, he thought, replacing the handset and trying again. He shouldn't give up so easily on the one who'd given him this wound; this was how he was supposed to feel – wounded. For a moment, he wanted to thank her for picking him out and making her mark on him, even if she'd done so in all innocence.

# Vixen in the Rain

In truth, those times when Dean caught up with Monika were as dispiriting as the times when he had no notion where she was. She'd fuck him, but not like before, mounting him and coming with chilling speed. There was an unfortunate evening when she refused even to remove her clothes – she was going out, she said. But still he begged to be let in, and they lay down together and had the most perfunctory sex, she a fully dressed Barbie and he a naked, plastic Ken, holding back the gusset of her knickers with his thumb while she kept an eye on her watch. He was so thankful to see her that he could have wept with relief, even as she fell away from him before the end and he spilled his seed on her sheets.

She was always on top and he was always underneath, watching her beautiful spine twist and weave in the ceiling mirror while looking for a sign in her green eyes, although daily they seemed to lose colour – a sign that she knew who he was or at least recognised him from somewhere. It was confusing, because she still looked just like the girl who'd given him her keys that first night, with the same hennaed hair, childlike elbows and clumsy feet, her skin's pallid glamour in the morning light. But she must be an imposter, a lookalike: where were those hints of something like gentleness, which once he'd taken for granted but now he craved? What had happened to her little shows of attention and that brief spell, when he was inside her, of calling out his name?

Fucking Monika only made him look harder for her when she was actually there, in front of him. Even when inside her, he missed her at every thrust, as if he could never get deep enough. On one occasion, when he plucked up the courage to complain about her cold and distant climaxes, she gave him a look of mild scorn. 'Sometimes I just want to have sex,' she said, 'and skip all the other stuff.' He cringed for himself, as if he'd made an unreasonable request – and it was unreasonable, of course, since he'd never made himself known to her in any way, revealed his thoughts or told her his feelings, told her that he liked it when she called him Dean. 'Okay,' he told her silently as he peeled off his pants and put out the light, 'so let's just have sex.' And then they writhed around like two drunken students playing Twister in the nude – but still it was not very satisfying, when what he longed for was a sign.

August span into September like a daytime somnambulist, walking through a series of bright afternoons with his eyes wide shut. One Monday evening after work, a golden evening with light sprinklings of rain, Dean made his way to Clapham on the Northern Line to seek solace from Laura, whose tolerance for his maudlin moods always touched him. But when he arrived at the end of her road, he realised that it made no sense to go on, when all he really wanted was to see his other lover. Retracing his steps to the scrubby plain of dry grass that was Clapham Common at the end of summer, he made a bargain with whatever perverse authority had first introduced them that if she were in and showed him some kindness he wouldn't ask to see her again. He smiled ruefully when he saw what he'd done. 'How superstitious I'm becoming,' he told himself, as he waited at the bus stop on Cavendish Road. But he caught his bus to Streatham Hill in the sureness that now she'd be home, now that he'd made his deal with the devil that wrote the book. He'd told his diary the night before that losing his waitress would be like a death sentence – and writing it down only made it more true. She could be cruel, but her cruelty kept him alive; she could be as cold as snow, but how that snow could burn!

Something about the evening, with its hints of autumn and ragbag of characters on the upper deck, reminded Dean of his childhood. He'd grown up not far away, in the bland environs of Dulwich Village where his parents still lived, impoverished in spirit but wealthy in mahogany and teak, the kind of people he'd spent a lifetime trying to avoid. It wouldn't have occurred to him to pay them a visit, or even to call. But riding the bus that evening, he remembered how, when he was a child, his mother would take him into town for a show. He recalled his childish wonder at discovering that ordinary Londoners could be as wacky as the characters in the plays they saw at the Aldwych, dressed in plastic sacks or old pieces of curtain fringed with lace, possessed by a garrulous madness. To distract him, she'd point out the Oval cricket ground or the Imperial War Museum, smiling as he clung to her arm – and for an instant it came back to him how much that woman had loved him.

The bus swept along suburban streets linking Clapham to Streatham Hill while nagging rays from a setting sun shone through the windows of the upper deck. London would never change. Tonight as he rode into the arms of his tormentor, he heard the incessant babbling of an old-timer who sat in the seat behind and rapped into the lapels of his gabardine mac. At first Dean assumed that the man was nattering to someone on the phone, but when he turned to look he saw that there was no phone, only a man with a face encrusted with scabs.

'The answer's yes, but you don't say where. Thank you, I enjoyed Saturday. I've got a little job for you. The answer's yes, but you don't say where.'

Unnerved, he switched seats, closing his eyes to a route that was, by now, engraved in his mind. It was a sort of homecoming to get down from the bus at Streatham Hill and walk up Leigham Court Road towards her redbrick hovel. The evening was as fair as the day had been; a rainbow spray fell from a cloudless sky, and the fragrance of wet city dust rose to his nose. On the pavement just ahead of him, a fox emerged from the gateway of a dilapidated villa – another little vixen, he thought, impossibly sleek and fashionably late. She went before him through the gloaming while he plodded along behind her in his Docs, heavy with yearning. Twilight began to draw its shadow lines along the rooftops, but the fox showed no unease; she glanced at him over her shoulder, nipped into a courtyard and vanished. Dean came to a halt, looking after her, where a mass of ivy covered the opening between two buildings. Foxes knew no fear, while rabbits froze in the sights of a farmer with his gun and froze, just the same, at the sight of a small boy with a toy pistol – and how, in his thirties, had he become such a rabbit?

Humberto opened the door and winked, and he felt his way down the dark corridor towards Monika's bedroom, where he found her propped up in bed, smoking, her paraphernalia scattered across the eiderdown and her fog filling the air. She was ill, or so she claimed – but she was forever shamming sickness. She must have called in sick almost as often as she went to work. Perched on the edge of her bed, he questioned her in his best physician's manner, foiled by her fits of giggles and abrupt lapses in concentration. She lay sprawled in her white jeans and black bra, as if she'd begun to dress for the evening but then been struck by a strange paralysis. Her symptoms were a headache, she said, and aches in other places, brought on by sexual starvation – it was nearly 48 hours since anyone aside from herself had given her an orgasm.

She said these things from time to time out of mischief, watching for his response, genuinely unaware it seemed that she didn't have to try to titillate him or turn him on. She didn't know – but how could she – that any desire he had for anything in the world found its object in her body; beyond her body, the world was nothing. Of course he was always exaggerating, and this was why no one ever believed him when he said this kind of stuff. But it was true nonetheless: she *was* sex, she *was* desire, there was nothing and nobody else. Sometimes when they were face to face at last he thought she might understand this, if he could explain himself; she'd felt that way about someone once, after all – she'd even told him so. But then just the fact of where they were, in her wreck of a room, with him so drunk or hungover and her so out of her head, made it impossible to utter the words.

Tonight she wasn't quite as stoned as she looked, however – only partly gone. 'Close the door, Dean,' she told him, falling back with an arm across her face.

He closed the door, took the joint from between her fingers and put it on the bedside table. Tonight there was something wistful about her, as if she'd spent the hours counting the days before the leaves would start to fall. He flung off his lumberjack shirt and stripped down to his boxers while she looked on without saying a word – but when he sat beside her and pulled her to him and kissed her, she kissed him back with such violence that it knocked him sideways. Thrown off balance, he banged his head on the shelf that was mounted crookedly above the bed, where she kept her glossies; back numbers of fashion magazines cascaded around them on the pillow and splashed behind the headboard – and for a while they were bombarded by her *Cosmos*, *Vogues* and *Harpers & Queens*.

Monika rolled her eyes and waved him on, in a knowing parody of empress and slave. She grabbed the joint from the bedside table and relit it as he peeled off her jeans, took down her knickers and stroked with the tip of his tongue the amazing crème brûlée of her cunt. Was it a crème brûlée, or was it a parfait? Metaphors flew from his mind as he sank his tongue into her box, where she was hot and sweet but never too hot to taste the sweetness, eating her out until her cream ran down the back of his throat. He was about to choke – but hell, what a happy death – when she shouted out some words in her own language and came with a tremor that shook several issues of *Marie Claire* to the floor. It was like her to keep on coming, this was just what she did: she clasped her breasts in her hands and thrust her hips upwards, where they made a circle in the fuggy air.

'Oh God,' she said, in English, 'oh God oh God oh God.'

And then they made love, and it was like the first time in its intensity and cinematic perfection – but tonight he felt something new. When he closed his eyes and felt her around him, felt her hold him inside her like a firm hand in a velvet glove, he experienced a shock of oneness, a jolt of intimacy. Even through the condom he felt every part of her around every part of him, like some perfect sync – and when he opened his eyes, he found her looking up at him, not just watching but taking him in, as if her look itself embraced him. She was *here*, he realised, in a stroke. He'd found her – the search was over.

It was by far the most terrifying moment of his life. In his terror he came at once and felt her come again – she let go on him with everything she had, a spurt of joy. In the moment they came together his head was swimming but he was drowning in feeling; even as his spunk ebbed out of him, he wondered whether he could drain himself of his fear, leave it all inside the rubber, chuck it in the bin. In that moment, he only wanted to fuck out of him what fucking had put there in the first place: a vision of her in relation to him that was as timeless as he'd first seen it, on that morning in Somers Town, but which didn't need to be timeless, could even have a timeline. This could be the start of something – it came to him involuntarily as they came together, and 'No, no, no,' came the answering thought, as he saw their life stretch out ahead of them, saw them walk hand in hand between pieces of furniture into a future with things in it, better things than they had now and the two of them side by side, together.

The last little bit left him and he threw himself down on the pillows, landing on a crumpled copy of *Elle*, which stuck to his shoulder blade until he sat up and tore it away. Other stuff seemed to fall away from them, slide from the bed to the floor – but then the room, normally so filled with sounds from other places, became for a minute extraordinarily quiet. He lay down again, and Monika lay beside him with her face turned to his, panting slightly and her chest still heaving, her green eyes holding him for a long instant before she laughed.

'You know what?' she said, grinning into his confusion, 'you drunk boys are really clumsy.'

There was another silence as she scrambled about for the joint, which they'd lost somewhere in the bedclothes, a silence that he knew he must exploit. He stayed her hand and held her fingers to his lips, licking her fingertips one by one, feeling her eyes on the top of his head. It had never struck him so clearly before how impossible it was to translate the inner to the outer. As soon as he opened his mouth, change would occur, but words could not dictate it – it could be any kind of change. A whisper meant as the first line of a poem could end up causing an earthquake.

'There's a party next week,' he told her, 'if you want to come.'

Monika pulled her hand away and fished the joint from a fold in the sheet. 'Really, Dean? You are asking me to go with you to a party?'

'Yes,' he said, 'I am, is that really so strange?'

'You mean that now you want to show me off to your friends?'

'Yes,' he said, watching her light up. Through her open window came a sudden gust of wind, the barking of a dog, the screech of rubber on tarmac. 'I do.'

Her eyes as they rested on him seemed to fill with a mix of irony and pity. 'Well then,' she said, 'that *is* new.' He shrugged, and she laughed; then waving her hand at him in her princess parody she said, 'Go, Dean. Go to the kitchen and make me a drink.'

He got up off the bed, looked around for his shirt and couldn't lay eyes on it. The room couldn't have been more disorderly if while they'd been fucking robbers had come in and hurled everything to the four corners, enraged to find nothing of value. He waded to the door through the piles of magazines and clothes. 'Lots of juice,' she called after him, 'lots of ice!'

In the kitchen, as he sought out the ingredients for a Screwdriver, Dean bumped into her landlord, who sat on the one very shaky chair and gazed out of the little window at the late dusk.

'Hey old man,' Humberto said, 'how's it going?' Dean shook his head and laughed as it struck him that he was wearing his boxers and nothing else and must reek of alcohol and sex. Humberto didn't seem to notice or mind. 'Are you looking forward to the 21st century? Think it's going to rock like this one did?'

'Oh,' said Dean, wrestling with the carton of OJ in his slippery grasp. 'I don't plan that far ahead. I guess I'll be a 20th century boy until I die.'

# Sparking Out

Laura watched the dancers from the stairs. Alberto was down there, twisting away with Carrie, whose neat form was encased in a silvery shroud that glimmered under the mirrorball their hosts had strung from the ceiling. Laura didn't want to dance or talk to her time-honoured friends, didn't want to be there, feeling hot and prickly in her dress – the heating was turned on, although it was still warm outside.

She wore the same purple taffeta dress she'd worn the last time she came to this house, the first time she met Dean. Down on the dancefloor, Alberto bopped about in his favourite shirt, a shiny black number he'd bought as a young man in the 1980s; it had gone with him from Pescara to the Big Apple and so on to London, moths disdaining its manmade fibres. She knew these things about her husband – and she knew that Carrie, who advanced towards him across the carpet, shaking her tiny tits in his direction, had always admired him for his density and gravity, lacking both herself. No doubt they would have made the better couple, if anyone had put two and two together, but life was never the result of such heady calculations.

And besides, by the time they met, people had already made their choices. Four years ago, on her return with Alberto from New York, when they'd all shared a flat together, he'd doted on Carrie, done her chores and picked things up from shops for her. It was kind of cute, she'd thought at the time. In those days, her husband was the only one in proper employment, hauling his immigrant ass out of bed at six while she slept in. She'd spent her many spare hours playing Monopoly with Carrie and Carrie's dunderhead of a boyfriend, eating tuna out of tins and chatting shit until her resourceful hubbie came home with dinner. At night they'd lie and listen to Carrie having sex through the wall, throwing herself at her idiot boy as if he were some sort of prince. It was already sad, she saw that now, but at the time it had seemed like a blissful break from reality before the struggle began, the long march to reach a standard of living in line with her expectations.

The song came to an end – something sinister and glacial by Massive Attack – and Carrie came to join her on the stairs while Alberto, with a glance towards them, went off in the direction of the kitchen.

'Aren't you going to dance, Loz?'

'Oh, I don't think so. I'm in a silent way tonight.'

'So why are you even here, babes?'

'Dean is meant to be coming. I don't see much of him these days.'

'I didn't think he came to parties.'

'He doesn't very often. I'm in my hopeless optimism mode.'

'Poor Laura. You got it bad.'

'Well, you know. If he was a normal person I could just forget about him, but he's too hard to define.' She glanced at her wristwatch, another memento from New York. 'If he was just a stud I could write him off and move on.'

Carrie laughed. 'Are you saying he's not that great in the sack?'

'He's not, actually. He's like what Hemingway's wives always said about Hemingway – you know, terribly abrupt. He cuts me off before I even get started. But maybe that's just the way he is with me. I dare say he's like fucking Casanova with the other one.' Laura lit a Silk Cut and held out the pack to Carrie. 'But I suppose you disapprove.'

Down on the dancefloor, in the hosts' immaculate lounge, a mellow Björk remix segued into *You're Never Alone with a Clone*. They'd hired a DJ, a friend of a friend who'd brought along decks and speakers and a mirrorball, a few red and blue spots. With all the houselights still on, the effect was overly genteel, as if the Bank of England had brought in a clown for a board meeting. Behind them on the landing, people in clothes denoting middle youth talked about the end of socialism and the function of spin. Beneath the sanguinity of these unthinking capitalists, she caught wind of a deeper complaint – a soft lament to the century's muddled finale.

'Come now, sweets, how could anyone disapprove of you?' Carrie stood, though standing made her seem no taller. 'I'll have to dance or I'll freeze to my rock.'

'Love your dress, Caz,' said Laura. 'You look like Edie Sedgwick at a school disco.'

'Wow, thanks old friend.'

When the tune ended, the DJ played *Get Get Down* and *Rendez Vu* and William Orbit's rocking beats version of Barber's *Adagio for Strings*, all so mindless and inane. She thought of taking herself off somewhere, maybe to the Patio on Shepherds Bush Green, where she'd buy herself a Goldwasser and read her placemat until something better came along; but her eye was drawn to a woman who danced by herself on the far side of the floor – but really danced, flicked her shoulders with no ironic withholding, a sincere shimmy in her white jeans. The houselights were turned down and the mirrorball twirled, throwing off primary colours, the DJ spinning now with zest, loud trickling streams of trip hop rolling through mountains of drum and bass. Laura would have fled this soundscape of mechanical squawks but for the woman in the white jeans and sleeveless top, the legend MILLENNIUM BUG across her chest.

She looked down at her glass of white Burgundy, gone warm in her hand; when she looked up again *Supersonic* was fading out into *Christiansands*, and the woman sat above her on the stairs. She turned and gave her a smile, and the woman smiled shyly back, shrugging and tugging at her bra-strap through her top, still panting from her exertions.

'You're a good dancer,' said Laura.

'What?' The woman leaned in, and Laura saw up close her green eyes with their wildly dilated pupils, high cheekbones and fabulous mouth. It was not that her lips were so full, but they were long – went the extra mile, heading for her dimples. It was a mouth that people would remember and talk about.

'I was watching you dance.'

'Oh, yeah. Well, I like dancing.'

The DJ played *Macarena* for a laugh, prompting uproar from the immaculate men with Norwegian sweaters tied around their necks and their pearl necklace partners. Several grumbling refuseniks left the floor in protest at the weakness of the joke. Laura went up one step to sit beside the girl with the mouth; anyone who wanted to get past would have to squeeze. 'Who do you know here?'

'Someone was supposed to meet me but I can't see him.' She shrugged again. 'And he doesn't have a phone. Well, he has a phone but he forgets to turn it on and leaves it around. He's very unreliable.'

Laura laughed. 'Do you want me to get you a drink?'

'Oh, no thanks. It's not my drug of choice.' She pulled a cigarette packet out of her purse and took out a pre-rolled joint. 'Want to share one of these?'

'Sure,' said Laura. 'Why not?'

They smoked, and from the very first drag everything shifted – the music made sense, the coloured lights made a magical matrix across the floor and walls and the woman in white jeans shed her skin and became translucent. The party started to make that strange threshing noise that parties make when they get into gear. Laura put her hands to her ears.

'This is really strong,' she said. '*So* strong.' Their heads were almost touching; she could smell the other woman's sweat. 'Really so strong.'

'I know,' she grinned, 'it's good grass. So what about you?'

'I came with my husband. He's down there somewhere, doing his thing.'

'I'm the odd one out,' the other woman said. 'Everyone else is so married.' She waved her hand at the crowd who flickered in the spots in the middle of the living room carpet.

'It's not a binary condition.'

'Pardon?'

'My husband is married to me but I'm not married to him,' said Laura. 'It's quite simple, but he still doesn't get it.'

'Poor guy.' The woman looked away, her face a mask of unhealed grief; then turning back to Laura she smiled, as if importing a smile from somewhere incredibly far away – and Laura in that instant saw who she was and why she could never have won. It was not just her mouth or her jeans; she had otherness in abundance like a sixth dimension, an effortless allure.

'But you have a boyfriend,' she said, carefully.

'I guess so. But I could never marry an Englishman. They are good in some ways. They can be funny and they understand society – they know how to be themselves, you know?' Laura nodded. She knew she was sitting in the wrong place and talking to the wrong person, but she was stuck on the stair as if nailed down, no way to move. 'They can be quite sophisticated,' she said, passing back the joint, 'but only in their heads. In their emotions they are just like little boys.'

Laura took a long drag and passed it back. 'I thought you had red hair.'

The woman stared at her, blinking. 'What are you saying?'

'He said your hair was red.'

*Zoo Station* kicked in then with its jagged roar, the theme came in, and the room seemed to leap as one. Monika looked at her with something welling in her eye. 'I let it grow out,' she said. 'This is my natural colour.'

'You don't know who I am,' said Laura. 'He doesn't know who you are. But I know who you are.'

Then the lights went out, the spots and lights on stairs and landing, and the music fell silent and left a weird resonance, like a silence that repeated itself.

Laura felt around her, but the other woman had vanished – but everything had gone into a darkness slashed in the back of her eyes with traces of white strobe and curlicues of red, blue and green, echoes of colour. She made her way down the stairs, pushing past soft bodies and hard surfaces that emanated little bleeps and signals, through the blackened and deserted kitchen and out into the garden. Out there in the natural light, things became clearer: a waxing three-quarter moon leaned among the stars, some dull and some bright, some battered and some as shiny as when they first appeared, all flashing on and off to the rhythm of her heartbeat.

She lay down at the end of the garden, in her old place beneath the lilacs and rhododendron. It was surprisingly quiet, all of nature in a lull; cats perched on fenceposts like watchtowers, sentries of their animal kingdom. There was a hint in the air of a coming chill, but only a little hint; people might have sat out on the lawn all night if they'd wished – but they preferred to press up against each other indoors, with no space between them. As her eyes adjusted slowly to the moonlight, she realised that someone was sitting at her feet, smoking and drinking from his hipflask. It was happening again, she thought – but she knew, even as she had the thought, that none of this would ever happen again.

She seemed to miss the start of her own sentence. 'Is it because she's foreign?' she heard herself ask. 'I can't do foreign, Dean.' Her voice echoed in her head, everything she said repeated and amplified into wild distortion, so she couldn't tell between what she'd just said and what she was about to say. 'I can't be a romantic exile, helpless in a strange land. I can't have problems with my visa, can't act like I've never known the barriers of money or class. I can't do *foreign*, Dean.'

She was crying, she realised from the vibrations in her face – she reached out and blew her nose on a rhododendron leaf. The house loomed over them, still dark from lack of power, like a ship full of ghost sailors, sailing treasureless back to an old continent where no one really wanted to live.

'No,' he said after a pause that might have been a minute or an hour, 'it isn't because she's foreign. It's not something you'll ever understand.'

'Then please don't try to explain.' Her voice tore into the night, seared the air and came back to her again, *explain*.

'First you want an explanation and then you don't. Which is it to be?'

'You invited her to the party. I can't believe you'd do something so cruel.' *So cruel*, she heard, *so cruel so cruel*, and for a second she felt the shock of hearing something not meant for her ears, as if she were eavesdropping on herself.

'Why do you think that?' He spoke in a tone of drunken indignation, sounding as he always did when he'd been caught out. Then he went quiet in the darkness, and she heard him drink again. 'Well okay, maybe I did – but she didn't come, did she?'

For a moment it was as if a switch was thrown in her head. Even in the murk of her own power cut she saw the crossed wires and had to fight an instinct to disentangle them – as if it fell to her to sort out all the confusions wrought by dope and alcohol. And she might have done so, if he hadn't gone on sitting there so calmly, smoking and drinking, oblivious. She couldn't give back to him what he didn't deserve.

'That's not the point. It was cruel to her as well as to me – but you don't think women bleed, do you? You think you can prick us as often as you want and we'll just scream into our pillows.'

'You're wrong,' he said. 'I know you have feelings.' He flicked his cigarette further into the bush, and it fell as slowly as a shooting star.

'It's our feelings you like to play with. To you we're all just elements in some experiment you're making on life. That's just what you do, Dean.'

'So you won't follow me any further,' he said, but with little sign of regret, as if she was a time-server announcing her long-awaited retirement. 'You can't handle the ride. You're calling me out on my spirit of adventure.'

'I'm calling you out on your heartlessness, you asshole.' She screamed the words into the midnight blue as it closed around her, airless and dense. Somebody moved in the kitchen doorway and shouted down the garden, 'Everyone okay out here?'

Neither said anything for a while; the ground beneath her began to feel chill, and she was about to try to rise and walk away when he spoke. 'I'll tell you why I love her, if you really want to know. I wanted a ticket out of here, and she's the one.' Laura heard the click of steel against his teeth, a hiss of brandy in the flask's neck, the cap rattling as it went back on. 'She's my death trip.'

'But you can die with me,' she said, in a voice she didn't recognise, full of passion and pathos, traveling the length of the garden and beyond, going out across the city. 'You can die with my hand on your heart – and it would *mean* something.'

She had his attention now, she knew; she saw his head turn, saw him look down. 'Your offer's kind, but I don't want meaning. I want to fly away and explode like a firework, with my head in flames, don't you see?'

Perhaps he hadn't said this – it seemed too extreme. She was about to ask him to say it again when suddenly he got up and began to move away. Her legs had no feeling and she couldn't stand to follow him, so she crawled after his blurred silhouette, casting around for words and finding none. His outline was about to blend with the house's shadow when every window suddenly blazed with light. The power failure ended in a white blast of flashing sound, flickers from the mirrorball carrying out onto the lawn, *Zoo Station* starting up again in the middle of a note, and every storey breaking out into a chorus of cheers. She made her way on hands and knees over the damp grass to the terrace edge, from where she could see into the lighted kitchen, and Dean standing there with his back to her.

'Well,' said the host, 'if it isn't Mr Quiet Desperation himself.'

'Hi Dean,' said the hostess. 'A girl was looking for you earlier.'

'How nostalgic,' said someone else, hidden by the door, 'a game of Hunt the Russler.'

There was a guffaw in response to this and a snickering, but Dean remained tied to the spot as if caught in an idea – she saw it in the way he stood rigid and clenched. A voice came from somewhere else in the kitchen, another blindspot, drawling, 'Wasn't she the one who left with Hugo?'

'Look at the poor guy,' laughed the host, 'he's all aquiver.'

'Like his liver,' someone else said – and everyone laughed, and Dean walked on through the kitchen and left.

Laura lay in the grass beside the terrace until the party died down, although it was a week after the autumn solstice and the grass was wet, and the ground after a while turned very cold.


# Apocalyptic Visionary


On the Wednesday after the party, Dean called in sick. The day was too impossibly bright and lonely and had too much wistful magic to waste a minute of it in the office, dipping into his book under the nose of the surly drab who was his boss, losing himself in filing, in the endless afternoon taking nips from his hipflask to while away the time. The thought of losing his job inspired no fear. There were other, almost identical jobs to be had in London that year, jobs with no ethical strings attached, which required him to do no harm, with only a tangential relationship to life as it was lived by ordinary people.

The night before he'd found himself in Kettner's with an old friend, where they downed two bottles of champagne between them before moving on to a basement bar in Greek Street. Slugging on his own most of a jugful of Margaritas, he'd put paid to what might have been a beautiful hangover, all bubbles and zest. Instead, he had the feeling that something had crumbled away inside him. At such moments he needed reassurance and a loving word, but this was also when he was forced to acknowledge that there was no one around to give him those things. So he thought instead that he'd call on his lover – and he left the flat at his third attempt, delayed by such small considerations that a minute later he'd forgotten them, and headed south.

He couldn't go to Monika for reassurance, of course. She didn't offer solace; far from it, she showed him the danger lying in wait behind every door. No doubt she'd be out and he'd have to wait all day for her return, and no doubt when she turned up she'd look at him as the red queen looked at Alice. But travelling and hanging around at least gave him something to work on while his head cleared. And then his memory of their sudden intimacy of a week ago remained with him, an instant that begged for repetition; it came back to him now and then, before he could push it away. He had no wish to know it for what it was. He knew there was never a good time to fall in love; for his own protection over the years he'd steered well clear of it – and not only for his own protection. He wouldn't want anyone to feel about him the way he felt about her, to be drawn into his dark little world.

He emerged at noon from the manic swell of the tube at Brixton. The streets pulsed with life under an Indian summer sun; people, cars and street furniture seemed to rise into the air on a tide of light. Rather than take the bus directly to Streatham Hill, playing for time he wandered up Acre Lane. It was still only mid-September; the leaves were still green, although the purple heads of buddleia had turned brown and the sun leered down from a tighter angle. The Brixton sun was brassy and raucous, clashed like a cymbal and throbbed in the air as people marched to its beat in an impromptu parade. Swaying ahead of him on the pavement, a shoeless man almost stepped on a dying wasp. He missed it by an inch, staggered to a low brick wall and took a hit on his tin of Carlsberg – and Dean smiled at him as he passed, hitching his satchel high on his shoulder. Not for the first time, he wondered why he lived in north London when he could be down here, in the chaotic embrace of the south.

He hooked a right, went up Raeburn Street and stopped at a house where only a year before, or was it two, he'd been a constant visitor. His memory was not what it was, but still he was fairly sure that the door had been yellow, and now it was red – and he was absolutely sure that Estelle didn't live here anymore. She'd only been renting; her life was as transient as his own. But as he crossed to the far side of the street and looked up at her window in the garret of the Edwardian terrace, he remembered her freckles and the mole on her chin and how her feelings always showed on her face. None of these things was lost, of course. He could bring it all back if he wanted to, could dig his memories out from under the bed where his diaries were kept.

A plain white butterfly, or perhaps it was only a beautiful moth, dipped past him to settle on a bush. He turned his back and walked away. In the gutter at the corner with Acre Lane he saw a penny, and out of habit he bent down to pick it up. Estelle was long gone; but she was alright, he told himself. She was out there somewhere, doing okay. He crossed his fingers and touched the dead buddleia where it sprayed across the pavement and put the penny in his pocket.

Glancing at his watch, he found it was almost lunchtime. It was no longer any good pretending that he didn't want a drink – and anyway he could think of no better place to sit on a day like this than Trinity Gardens. He sat on a bench in the forecourt of The Trinity Arms with a pint of Youngs and a packet of peanuts, overlooking the little square with its plane trees and the children's playground. He watched dust rise, swirled into life by occasional passing cars, and drank to quell the feeling that surfaced with each sip. He was almost 33, he couldn't think of himself anymore as young – but on a day like today, so bright and empty and full of spare hours, when no one was around to persuade him otherwise, he seemed to be travelling at full speed towards the person he'd been a decade ago. He admired and pitied that brash kid for his artlessness and naivety – that boy of summer, who played Risk all weekend at a house party where he overstayed his welcome by 24 hours, and knew it and stayed anyway, content with crumbs from the carpet and leavings in the kitchen, careful to show no pain when his girlfriend was swept off her feet by someone with a stronger sense of purpose.

He raised his hand in greeting to his younger self, who sat at the next table with a fringe full of hair, his eyes so clear of doubt, drinking as if there was no tomorrow. It was a happy reunion; he was glad to see himself again, so feckless, reckless and undismayed – but then it was hard to meet his own eye. How could he explain away those intervening years, or the way he lived now: how he'd spent the summer trekking between two women, neither of them truly his, how he worked in an office on the lowest rung, just as he had when he was 22, how he lived in rented rooms with nothing to show for it all but a tower of vinyl and a pile of debts and a million words of unpublishable prose? The office and debts and aimless attachments – these were the motifs of 1999, as they had been of 1989, the year when he graduated, and all the years that came between.

As if on cue, a couple of guys of student age came out of the pub and sat on the nearest bench. In their blue stonewash jeans and white t-shirts they projected an image of macho cool. When one of them glanced him over with chilly disdain, Dean became aware of the antiquity of his uniform – his pale chinos turned white with age, his holey Docs, a lumberjack shirt washed so many times that the sleeves stopped short of his wrists. But then on Acre Lane a car backfired, for a few seconds all the birds in south London seemed to lift into the air, while from the jukebox inside the bar Rod Stewart sang *You Wear It Well*. Not even the presence of the two smirking youths could impinge on this painfully beautiful Indian summer afternoon. But Jesus how he envied them their unused potential, energies not misspent on bad trips or misspelled résumés or piles of letters left unsent, or his trail of broken hearts. They wouldn't waste years in pointless toil, invisible work that didn't need to be done, so he couldn't even say *Not through me!* They wouldn't use up their leisure hours dancing to *Temptation* again and again and again, or wanking over the same paragraph by Anaïs Nin – no, they'd apply themselves and make good.

Dean took a book from his satchel, but the brown swill of beer inside his skull made it hard to focus on the page, and he closed put it away and sloped off to the bar to fetch another pint. Why not get as drunk as humanly possible? What else was there for him to do in this hard land, strewn with eyesores and low rises and ruled by a thousand snobberies? So he sat on and an hour passed and then another hour, the young men left and a group of nurses took their place at their table, and he drank until the sun fell below the roofline and the air turned cold and everyone else went indoors.

Under a moon almost full he pulled himself to his feet, and as if struggling with some nameless weight began to climb the slow incline, walk the two miles to Monika's pad. The way up Brixton Hill was heaving with shadows and loud with blaring horns; sole pedestrians weaved on cracked paving stones past shuttered shop fronts like people with no mission but to survive, a vision of a world that was nearly over. All this flickering menace recalled a time in his youth when he was in love with the notion of the world ending, even while it filled him with terror. In those days, it was a form of paranoid entertainment to look forward to the closing credits; he would watch them roll with a mouthful of magic mushrooms, walk hand in hand with his chosen stranger towards the exit sign.

Reaching the brink where Brixton Hill became Streatham Hill, faced with the brokedown palace of The Crown and Sceptre, he was sorely tempted to stop in and have another pint. But he pressed on down through grungy tenements, between 1930s blocks with metal windows and sightless facades, swerving from gutter to wall, walking splay-legged as if he'd soiled himself and avoiding the eye of anyone in his path – streetwise girls in hotpants, shopkeepers on stoops and drunkards dangling tins. All at once he found himself blushing from a shame so overwhelming that it itched his scalp and ached his spine, filled his shoes like rain. There was no help for it now, but a vitality had gone from his insights into things. He was subjective, but not like before – his vision of the apocalypse, once so vivid and real, had dwindled to a facile hopelessness.

Arriving at Leigham Court Road, he couldn't find his key, but Humberto opened the door to him. It was strange, but tonight the landlord looked almost handsome, in a way that Dean would have liked to be – handsome and serious, handsome and kind. 'She's not here, man,' Humberto said, letting him in.

Dean tripped over the threshold into the corridor with its bare bulbs and essence of marijuana. 'Oh well, never mind.' He looked at his friend hopefully. 'You've got some vodka hidden away somewhere, yeah?'

Humberto held out a steadying arm. 'She's gone, man. She left.'

The landlord led him through to her bedroom, stripped of all female accoutrements, the bed now bare of its sheets and showing a mattress marked with bizarre and elaborate stains. In a pantomime of a search, Dean opened the wardrobe door and even the tallboy, finding only the extent of their emptiness. After a minute of this, he sat down on the bed. 'Oh fuck,' he said. 'Oh Jupiter.'

'She didn't call you to say she was going?'

'Going where?'

Humberto stood in the doorway, handsome and serious. Falling back on the bed, Dean caught a glimpse of himself in the mirror before he closed his eyes.

'I'm not exactly sure, boss. Back to Europe, maybe.'

'Or maybe to another shitheap like this one.'

'Yeah, maybe another shitheap like this one.' Humberto stood over him, clearing his throat. 'Shall I go buy some vodka? Stay here tonight, why not, looks like there's a spare bed.'

'Oh my God.' Dean sat up and crossed the room and pushed off the walls down the corridor to the door of the flat, falling over his feet. 'Really, we had a great time.'

'I know. She was hot, man. I'm sorry.'

'No. I mean you and me, Humberto.'

The landlord smiled his sad smile, holding his eye. 'You need to sit down perhaps,' he suggested. 'You look kind of dangerous right now.'

Dean laughed, choked on his phlegm and spat through the open front door, then followed his spit out onto the walkway. He laughed and choked again, holding out his two clumsy paws as if miming a hug, but already backing away.

'Yes, yes, goodbye, Humberto.'

# Brandy Alexanders

By the time Laura saw Dean again it was the middle of October. The Indian summer had cracked down the middle and let in the drizzles and downpours that would last until March or April. He came to visit her one evening, out of the blue – she opened the door to him. As he stood in the hall, shaking the rain from his hair like a dog, it struck her that this was a Dean much altered from the man she'd met at the start of summer. His hairline had receded so far that the knobs on his forehead stood out clear. His temples were exposed, his arms seemed shorter and his back less straight. He trembled, from cold or alcohol, and the look on his face was one of worn patience.

Alberto wore a similar expression, of course, but her pity for Dean was greater. Her husband drifted into things, let them mess him up and then complained about the consequences. Dean had decided to junk himself on a girl and driven hard towards the rocks – and now he stood before her, cradling the broken pieces of himself, she could almost love him for that alone. There's a special kind of sympathy for those who break their own hearts.

For the same reason, however, she didn't really want him in the house that evening. He was too pale and shaky, and she was painfully aware that his pallor and trembling had nothing to do with her. As he began to take off his coat, she suggested they go out somewhere.

'What,' he said, 'in this rain?'

'Are you scared of a little rain, Russler?'

So they went out and walked an ungainly stretch of Clapham High Street arm in arm, while traffic flung up plumes of water from the gutters. As she walked beside him, their bodies barely touching, she felt how drenched he was and how porous; if he was still wet through this way when winter came, all the water inside him would freeze and he'd split apart. It was strange, because he was only a year older than her, but he was already too old for the game he'd been playing. She thought of what Sagan says at the end of *A Certain Smile* – 'I was alone, I'd loved a man, it was no big deal.' But the heroine was only 21, when nothing was too terrible, too soon or too late. For Dean perhaps it was too late: he'd travelled back in time to revisit some earlier version of himself and to recreate the mindless passion he might have known in his twenties, gone back and found the place far lonelier than he'd expected. She knew this about him, put it together from hints and guesses – but she knew, too, that there was nothing she could do for him now.

When the downpour became more intense, they slipped into a bar with windows for walls so the street lay exposed to their gaze, crowded with men and women of around their own age, who perched like them on chrome and leather-look stools at little round tables. Dean smoked tab after tab and talked incessantly as the night outside turned wetter and blacker. Now and then she tried to divert him, draw his attention to funny things about this clean, well-lighted place where they sipped their cocktails, but her words could only check him for a second.

'I even went to see my mother,' he said, gazing not at her or the room they were in but at the black, wet street through the window.

'Your mother? Really, why?'

'I suppose I thought she'd rock me in her arms and tell me everything was going to be okay.'

Sipping from her glass, she held her upper lip under for an extra second, then licked off her cream moustache with the tip of her tongue – a thing she always did with Brandy Alexanders. Other men in previous eras had found it adorable, or so they'd said. 'I can't imagine your parents. Do they look like you at all?'

'My dad was sitting out on their horrible patio in his deckchair with a blanket over his knees and his pipe and his bottle of gin. Honestly, he looked like something that escaped from an old people's home, or a corpse laid out for dissection. I felt like taking a knife to him.' Dean paused in his rant to count his change, piling his pound coins on the table between them. It was one of his more irritating habits – like a marker for his poverty, as if he had to remind himself how little was left. All year she'd wanted to tell him to stop, stop, for God's sake stop – but for that, too, it was too late. 'I only go around there once a month at most, but every time the old man gives me the same lecture. Can you guess what it is, his idée fixe?' She shook her head, but his gaze was directed elsewhere. 'He can forgive me for my second class degree and my bank balance and the Horlicks I've made of my life, but he's never really forgiven me for burning a hole in his lawn when I was 17.'

'Ah,' she said, licking her lip and gurning at him, 'how well I remember those teenage barbecues.' But Dean was busy putting the coins back in his skimpy wallet.

'I must have looked extremely hungover because when I was leaving mum asked me how I was – something she would never normally do. I was feeling so fucking dreadful that I told her the truth, I told her my heart was breaking. You know what she said?'

'Something about the tin man, perhaps?'

And she laughed, but Dean went on, immune to her tone. 'She said that if it was over a *boy* she wanted to be the first to know, she didn't want to find out from her *neighbours* that I was *gay*. I quote her exact words.'

'Wow,' said Laura. 'Is she always that subtle?'

'So I said that yes, I'd fallen in love with a hunk of a guy with a shitload of tattoos but he'd run off with someone younger and prettier. And you know what, I think she even believed me.' Dean put his glass down on his lighter, where it wobbled perilously for a second – but he snatched it up again before it could fall and wiped away the gobbet of

184

cream that splashed his chin. 'Silly old cunt, it's always such a mistake to let her in.'

'Poor Dean,' sighed Laura, looking past his shoulder at the smart people out on their Sunday dates – smarter, at least, than the date she was on – lifting their glasses and toasting their futures with impunity, keeping the world at bay with laughing eyes. 'You men are really stuck with your mothers, aren't you? You can't just dump them like you would any other woman.'

'Oh, I've dumped her alright. She can cut me out of her will if she wants, but I'm never going back to that fucking house.' He snorted indignantly, as if someone had accused him of being cynical and mercenary. 'I'm not cosying up to them for the sake of my inheritance.'

'Hardly worth it I shouldn't have thought, for a pipe and a bottle of gin and a lawn with a hole in it.' He glanced at her crossly, then looked away and lit another cigarette, although the room was already full of smoke; she watched it break up into little grey clouds through the motion of people across the room. 'I'm sorry if I'm not making the right noises, Dean, but I can't really go with you on all this mother-hating stuff. I mean, I might be a mother myself one day.'

He gazed at her then in disbelief, as if she'd just broken into Mandarin – but then in that instant he was back, laughing at his own reaction, the Dean of old. 'So why don't you do the talking for a while?' he said. 'Where are you going, anyway?'

'I'm going to the toilet, if that's okay.'

'No, it's not okay. You know I can't stand myself alone right now.'

She stopped off on her way back from the bathroom for another pair of Brandy Alexanders. Rain showed in silvery dots against the tinted glass that shielded them from the bleak externals. As she crossed the floor, a flicker caught her eye; outside on the pavement, an ageless and sexless being with a straggly mane wrestled its way into a black plastic bag, pushing its arms through the homemade armholes. Dean was watching too – she saw him shrink from this vision of homelessness. But when she came over with the drinks he looked up and smiled in his old way.

'So tell me how it is,' he said, 'with my Laura.'

'Nothing to tell. Same old story of a Latin control freak and a silly country girl.' She leaned across and lit for him the cigarette that had been dangling unlit between his lips for some time. 'You know, Dean, I've always loved listening to you talk. It's been my favourite thing about this year.' Putting down the lighter, she covered his cool hand with her own.

'You're not going to bite me now, are you?'

'You seem gravely bitten as it is, Dean.'

'Oh,' he released his hand and threw it in the air theatrically. 'It's a scratch, a mere scratch, I shall recover in time.' His frown made deep creases in his forehead, lines that hadn't been there at the start of summer. 'But why do we go through all this shit again when we already know how it ends?'

'Don't be such a goat, Dean. You love the crazy yo-yo effect. You love the pain of the chase and the thrill of defeat – you need it to feel alive. You'll always be like that.'

'No, I won't, sweetheart. You see, I'm going to change.' He drank, nodded to himself, blew on the lighted end of his fag as if to radiate conviction. 'That was the whole point of this Monika gig – it showed me how desperate we all are, at the end of the day. When we get to our age, it doesn't matter what we do – we can write the great American novel or start an import-export business or discover a cure for cancer, but we're all just filling in time before we die.' She made another cream moustache, rolled her eyes and blew a smoke ring, but Dean clung to his script. 'Shake your head if you like, but it's true. If I hadn't met Monika when I did, I might have lived up in cloudland a little while longer. She revealed the essence of things, I owe her that one. And now I know the truth, I shall live my life accordingly, whatever that means.'

He picked up his glass and drained it in one gulp. Aspects of his being protested at the sudden influx of brandy, nutmeg and crème de cacao; she saw it in his bugged-out eyes, the way he lurched forwards in a silent belch and gripped the seat of his stool with both hands. His eyes slid from her face to the street, where the lights of stalled cars blurred in the rain.

'Now you're worrying me a little, Dean,' she said. He looked back at her absently while she swizzled her stick in the dregs of his drink. 'It's just too decadent to see us as desperate, you know. We only toy with despair because we have too much time on our hands – that's all. Monika is an obstacle you ran into along the way. You can walk away again, Dean. Believe me,' she reached over and finished his drink for him, 'I know where you've been.'

Dean shrugged and fired his burning butt absentmindedly at the floor, his eyes on the table between them, vacant again. The London night had plateaued, and they were stuck out on the plain; they had at last run out of things to say to each other. The waiter came over with more to drink, but Dean only stared at his glass in a fit of abstraction, plucking out his icecubes and dropping them into the ashtray. In the end, she took his hand again and kissed his palm, and he drew away and winced.

'There's something a little sad about this conversation.'

'I know,' he said. 'I'm sorry I've been such a bore.'

'You never bore me, Dean. Remember, I live with someone who talks about his conjugal rights.'

'You should have married somebody like me,' he laughed. 'Someone with a bit of moxie.'

'I know,' she said, taking his hand again and holding on this time. 'We have a genius together, don't we? I felt it from the start. Tell me you felt it too, or I'll know you're lying.'

'I know what you mean, Laura. We have a genius, we have a rapport. We have timing and panache.'

'Alberto married me and then laid me to rest, kind of thing, prepped me for a quiet middle age. You wired me up and span me round and got me going again. I appreciate what you did, Dean.'

They sat for another minute or two without speaking, and in the loud and overheated bar they were for a moment its still, calm centre. In the end, they let each other go, polished off their drinks and stepped out into the rain. Cold water blew from the north into their faces, making them shudder; they walked on until they reached the shelter of the Underground at Clapham Common. As they came to a halt beneath the concrete awning, Dean seemed to brighten.

'Hey, do you remember the afternoon when we lay on the grass behind The Windmill and you told me about the piano? You remember that time?'

'Don't get us started on some memory trip, Russler. We're better than that – and I'll lose it if you do.'

He coughed into his sleeve, avoiding her eye – his satchel hung from his arm, its leather dark with rain, all its secrets unrevealed. Even standing in the shelter of that concrete lip, he seemed to channel the downpour; it ran from his eyebrows and down his fingers as he held out his hand to her, so that their handshake was a wet clasp. 'I guess we'll always have Clapham,' he said feebly.

'It's alright,' she said, 'we've done all our jokes, you don't need to get quippy.'

A flower seller appeared beside them then in a green canvas cape, grinning broadly as if delighted to stumble on two lovers. He held out a bucket of roses, red petals blanched by ambient fluorescence.

There were only two left, and Dean took one and handed the guy one of his pound coins; as the seller swam back into the night, he held it out to her.

'Isn't it cool that I bought you a flower, though? Maybe even funny?'

'No,' she said, 'not cool and not funny.' But she took it from him all the same, then took a step backwards into the dank street. 'Time to go home – and don't look so bewildered, man. This is the start of something new. Just screw your courage to the sticking place. You know the drill.'

Dean gave her a look of sad enlightenment. 'We can change our minds about life, don't you think?'

'Yes, I think we can. It takes some work, but it's possible.'

'It's just a shame we can't change our hearts.'

He turned then and went over to the steps that led down to the platform, a bedraggled scarecrow in his old tweed coat, and started down. She watched him go with his hair flattened to his scalp, his trousers stuck to his calves, his shoulders braced against the breeze – and that was the last she ever saw of Dean Russler.

She walked home through the deluge to find Alberto on the pea-green couch in the living room. He looked so cosy there and self-possessed that she had an urge to back away and leave him to his own devices; but of course she lived there too, she had nowhere else to go. He'd made dinner, a very palatable lasagne, and had opened a bottle of wine, which they shared like old times. She ate with one eye on the TV news and the other on her husband, who now and then turned to glance at her quizzically. Her rose stood on a low table between them in a vase, more the idea of a rose than a real flower, since it had lost a lot of petals in transit. She'd throw it away in a day or so – but still, it was a nice touch. She returned her husband's quizzical glance with a smile; neither of them spoke, except to comment on the weather. It was the kind of night in that they might have had at the start of their marriage – sitting side by side in companionable silence, two hearts beating almost as one.

# The Recluse

For a month that seemed to last a century, Dean cried for his waitress. Every night he fell on his knees on the filthy carpet and wept until he could barely remember why he'd started crying, beating on the windowsill with his fists while cars flew down Camden Road and midnight crackled with electric pain. It was agony of a magnitude – and in his more lucid minutes, leaving for work in the morning or closing the office door behind him at five, he could admit to himself that he'd never experienced anything like it before.

Throughout that dire October, he was appalled over and over by his vulnerability. He'd failed to take into account how deep his wound was, how little he knew how to heal it, and while he did his best to ironize – *Oh, Romeo is bleeding*, he sang to himself – singing did no good, irony did no good. Every night he woke up gasping for air, fell out of bed and struggled to the window with its broken sash, held his head between his knees and tried to breathe through his tears. Knowing that his tears were real, he felt asphyxiated. It was as if an invisible Monika had made her way into his bedroom and put her hands around his throat. Some nights he fell asleep on his floor and woke in darkness, in a breathless panic, hoping to see her above him and find her the cause of all this breathlessness, longing to find her fingers digging into his flesh, her vast indifference transformed into murderous rage. Oh why could she not just come around and kill him? But she wouldn't, he knew that really – and in any case she couldn't, because she had no idea where he lived.

At the end of those four weeks, he had a dream that captured her at her finest – her pale thighs, her sweet and salty sex. But in this dream her once bewitching effect, whatever had caused the sky to darken and his body to contract in longing, was no longer there. He awoke with a moan to find himself lying as if in a tomb, his hands folded across his chest, sunlight peeling the wallpaper in the corner above his bed. On that bright Monday morning on the first day of November, he opened his eyes to find the pain had left him and he was alone, with only a blank space and a mist where his longing had been. He was, at last, *over* the Moldovan.

As autumn lengthened into winter, he slipped into an almost puritan regime. Even if it rained, he swam before work at the lido on Endell Street, and after work he went swimming again, towards a sun that set between towerblocks overlooking the pool. November was brisk; his body stopped a chill wind – steam rose from the water, backlit by pool lights. But he stripped off in the gorgeous mantrap of the Oasis changing rooms, held an invisible gun to his head and made himself jump in at the deep end. At least in the water he was warm and wet, even if the breeze turned his hair into an icy skullcap.

Afterwards he ate at Picasso's or the Chelsea Kitchen on King's Road or the Portobello Star, drank his rum and coke, eavesdropped on the idle rich and wrote his diary. From the vantage point of a table by the door, he watched the street pass by until it was time to go home, when he walked halfway to Camden through nights that were crisp and cold but mild and full of peace.

That November he began to wander again – out of habit, since he was no longer looking for Monika, with only a dim memory of the feelings that had inspired all his toings and froings in the summer. Only time spent between the four walls of his flat recalled those days of far-off August when he was always on the hunt – always exhausted, frowning just to keep himself awake. Some of that turmoil clung to their blistered paint, yellowed with nicotine, and whenever he got back after midnight and shivered under the bare bulb in his living room, he thought of moving. But he had too many books, too much vinyl; shifting all those boxes downstairs – and upstairs too, no doubt – was not a winter task but one for spring, perhaps. So he went home as little as possible, until it felt as if he hardly lived there at all.

He skipped the Underground, spurned buses and walked for hours from where he drank to where he slept, crisscrossing the zones at random. Nights were coal-black but full of silvers and greys; faces came towards him after sundown like small circles of warmth. He walked down to the river and stood beneath Millbank Tower, gazing up at the two beams of light that sprang from the roof and met in the sky. A jogger slowed to catch the time from Big Ben while a helicopter hovered over Westminster. 'And if you think I see some special significance, Horatio, in those two beams of light – well I do, I do, I do.' As he walked, he talked to himself, loitering on the old Hungerford Bridge, listening out for music that played in the Purcell Room, as if its strains might drift upstream. He moved on after a minute, in the knowledge that if he stayed there long enough a gang of youths might come and throw him into the water – and there to float, and there to drown. He went south past Lambeth Palace to the Elephant, through darkness stained orange from sodium lamps, alone but for Horatio and his visions. But oh, the smell and taste of the streets at night, the flavour of those epiphanies!

Once he'd thought of London in winter as just a chilly space filled with dead leaves, but now he didn't mind the cold and emptiness, feeling its dark immensity like walls of a vast room he could explore forever, with no fear of boredom. The capital opened up to show him Georgian squares hidden away in Southwark's shabby expanses, discoloured mansions with weeds that grew from gutters. He stopped before the windows of an African dressmakers on the Walworth Road, then sat outside a café to watch the planes begin their descent like Chinese lanterns through the fuggy air. In those precious minutes of absorption the self he knew, the *Dean* he wrote about in his diaries, ceased to trouble him or even to exist as anything other than an eye cast on an invisible city, the walking eye he was bound to be.

Main routes and alleyways, park gates and other portals answered his call for something out of the ordinary and gave up their magic to him as to one properly initiated. One evening he saw a girl fly across the Old Kent Road on a pogo stick, heedless of traffic, zipping between cars with a look of out-there bliss. On a rush-hour Friday on Camberwell Green, a man with wiry grey hair stood balanced on one foot, in a dancer's pose. Dean stopped and looked back and stood there for a minute, but the man's expression never changed; he stood motionless, gazing at something in mid-air concealed from everyone else, until an impatient woman bumped into him with her bags. A pack of dogs one drizzling Sunday emerged from an alley near Chelsea Wharf and crawled one by one through a gap in the fence to an abandoned warehouse, as if they had a plan and were sharing with him if not the plan itself than at least one stage of its execution. All November, London yielded up its endless stream of otherness, in which he was simply another piece of flotsam.

## Snow Leopards

Of course, he asked himself now and then where they all were, the other Deans – because there were others, he knew; he was not unique. He'd heard about them on the grapevine, overheard people at parties say things that he was sure they also said about him. Perhaps he'd even seen them across crowded rooms at those same parties, through the sea of men with time and money. And of course, he was curious – he wondered about them when he read about them in books – but now even the other Deans seemed to give him a wide berth, and he was left alone with his sole courtier on his solitary maunderings. 'So this is what it's like, Horatio, really to be a recluse.'

In his heart of hearts, he knew it wouldn't last; even during the belle époque of his reclusiveness, he filled his diary with sentences full of yearning, vivid descriptions of a life he was fated to return to. But for a month or more his life went by this way, in slow but constant motion, as if it was important not to stand still for too long or he might start to question his direction. Now and then he reassured the vaporous ally at his side, 'Those who crash their car on Victory Road must walk the extra mile to Defeat Street.' But his defeat no longer grieved him, and tonight he didn't mind walking. In the last weeks of the year came a kind of hush, like the murmur of people at a secret gathering, hiding behind a door and waiting for the right moment to leap out and yell, 'Surprise!' There was this sense of expectation, but no sense of time; because he'd lost touch with everyone, there was no context to any of these experiences and he no longer felt his true age – but it felt like the last winter of his youth, even so. Soon he'd begin his decline, a thought that came to him sometimes as he walked. There was even a rattle in his chest when he breathed, although it may only have been the bottle tops in his breast pocket, shaking as he went. But as long as he could inhale he would smoke, as long as he could swallow he would drink, and at the times when he was sitting still he did both to extremes.

He drank on a barstool in Inverness Street and breathed in the heady scent of lime and mint that went into his vodka gimlets, downing one after another until he saw far into the future, or nothing at all. It wasn't that he was looking for an end to things; he was at peace in those days at the start of December, as if he'd come to a shelter between trees in his mental forest. Alcohol kept him there, in that peaceful place; each shot was instead of a kiss, because now he knew what a kiss could do and knew to have shots instead. He watched how other men were with their women on Saturday nights on Underground platforms, in cinema foyers and at restaurant tables, predatory and craven, doting and cajoling. He must have been all those things over the years – but all he really remembered was how a woman could always see through him, if she bothered to look. She'd take him in at a glance and be willing to sleep with him for a night or a week or a month, closing her eyes to everything but his mouth but closing her ears to what it said.

One evening he stopped to look at his reflection in a shop window in Regent Street, arrested by a thought: what *had* they seen in him? His face was like an open invitation to lie back and forget. His eyes were too lit up with their own games to inspire trust, his mouth had made the rounds once too often to be taken seriously. But none of them had taken him seriously, after all; they'd fed on his cock then left his side without a second thought. He raced away from Racing Green, shaking the image from his head, telling himself that none of it mattered anymore. He was content as he was, unseen and untouched, the cat who walked by himself. The world was just a show put on for his pleasure, and he'd always loved it that way – and the world had loved him back by handing out phenomena for free, because he observed so closely the way it turned, its *son et lumière*. So they might sit and admire each other until the very last day, the world and Dean Russler.

By the end of November, the streets had turned as dank as a windowless abattoir – a London dankness, diesel fumes and that ashtray effect, some noxious effluence from flues of fast-food places, all held down by the anticyclonic flow. He tried to look ahead and imagine how glorious it would be again at the start of a new season, but it was hard to look forward from gutters that were streams of dirt or the paper-strewn wilderness of his living room. Instead he looked back to the spring just gone, which had brought with it Monika and Laura, when he saw the river every day from bridges and sang the song each time, of how he 'made a brooch of Somers Town'. His recollections were so vague though, as if he'd spent that whole period gazing at one feature of one person, seeing the rest with blinkers on. Yes, there was the Thames beneath him and the flicker of light seen from trains, an endless series of hellos and goodbyes – a sense of some continual aftermath, a relentless pathos. Monika herself seemed so utterly unknowable in retrospect, as if his knowledge of her stopped after that first night, or even in the Turkish casino after the first time she smiled.

In stale December rain he hung about Kings Cross, longing to lie down with one of the prostitutes who sometimes sidled up to him, always addled by drugs and scarily out of it. But he told himself that it wasn't ethical or romantic, he'd only be adding his problems to theirs. In an ideal world, of course, he'd have talked a woman into going to bed with him for free – but he had too little zip left in him to charm the pants off a passing stranger, and he couldn't bring himself to dip into his little red book. There was Estelle, of course. But there'd always been Estelle; it was as if her existence for him extended far into the past, to long before he'd met her, all the way back to his adolescence. She hung somewhere at the back of all this, a portrait on a wall never fully explained, a story he'd never told himself properly. She seemed to him oddly more substantial than ever, and when he thought of her now she returned to him vividly in every facet: her smell, how she pushed him away, her loud and ludicrous laughter. But even if he'd known her address, he wouldn't have written to her. His old flames belonged to the past – and if he had one fear greater than all others, it was the fear of repeating himself.

Restlessness drove him down into town. Behind Holborn station, he stumbled on a place called Na Zdrowie, where he let the swish of Slavonic voices sweep over him while drinking shot after shot of Żubrówka, a clean hit that left him feeling luminous and inert. He watched them as they talked, central and eastern women: Czechs and Slovaks, Latvians, Lithuanians, Poles, Ukrainians, Byelorussians and Russians. Fine-boned or statuesque in their white jeans and fake fur collars, they reminded him of snow leopards he'd seen as a child at the zoo. Each sat in her circle of admirers while toms brought her titbits; she'd climb to a higher branch for her feline contemplation then climb down again to play. He would have liked to take one home and be flayed alive by her claws, but he could never get to the snow leopards through their pride of polite and intelligent men.

After nights of watching women in the Polish bar, he was torn between drawing attention to himself in some way and going back to his solitude. After all, it had been wonderful to be a recluse. But the snow leopards barred his way, making it hard to leave until time was called – and by then he was too moiled in drunken fascination to do anything but retire to the toilets and pull at his dick. Folded up on the floor against the bowl he fell asleep and was eventually woken by a barman; he left in a blind rush, forgetting his old tweed coat, worn for nearly fifteen years and loved as much as any person. He didn't even miss it until he was almost at his door, when he found himself trying to roll a cigarette without a Rizla. Frozen on the corner of Camden Road and Lyme Street, he asked anyone who passed for a paper – and it must have looked as if he were begging or cruising, but he really didn't care. After all, there's no substitute for a Rizla, unless you have scissors and glue, an old copy of the Evening Standard and a heart entirely inured to squalor.

The next day was Christmas Eve – it had crept up on him, Christmas, and now suddenly it was white again, crisp again. He called in sick, bought a new coat from the market and refilled his hipflask with brandy. In a week's time it would be the new year, and then he'd begin again from scratch, with an open mind. The passion he'd felt for Monika had passed, was dead and gone, but someone or something was bound to come and take her place – no matter who or what it was, it didn't even have to be a snow leopard. Flicking through the pages of his diary that afternoon before setting out, he gave this period a name in a script made bold by overwriting several times with his gel pen: **Anyone Who Catches My Eye Can Have Me**.

## Dean and Alberto

On Christmas Eve, at twilight, Dean came out onto Long Acre and fought his way through the end of year crowds. He was about to cross and head towards Covent Garden piazza when he saw Alberto approach on the other side of the road, wearing a large black coat that dwarfed him and an equally ridiculous fedora. Dean turned his back and took in the plastic trees in the windows of Marks & Spencer, sprinkled with their permanent snow, and reflected in the glass a silver man, a unicyclist and a fiddler, the parade of late shoppers. Imposed on this background was his own slouching figure, with an unshaven face and unwashed hair, the replacement coat and his white shirt with its dirty collar. He would have closed his eyes to it all, but something made him look, and he took in every detail of his last evening as himself.

Alberto tapped him on the shoulder, and Dean turned to face him – and suddenly he was glad to see the guy, if only because he brought back those months with Laura. The other man eyed him with dull suspicion – no doubt, he thought, they were both thinking the same thing. But it wasn't the same thing, because her husband had no idea what a gem he possessed. Even her friends knew only the Laura who chopped and changed between brittleness and satire, who made her snarky remarks then gazed off into the middle distance. He was alone with the memory of her occasional brilliance, the madness of her skin.

'Hiya, Dean,' said Alberto, removing his silly hat and wiping his glasses on his sleeve.

Dean looked beyond the Italian to the colonnade, where bodies hurtled to and fro. 'Well how about this for a meeting of minds. I took the afternoon off,' he added, as if he owed Alberto an explanation.

'So did I,' admitted Alberto, sullenly. 'Now we're here, why not let's go for coffee?'

'Alright.' He made a show of glancing at his watch. 'I've an hour or two before I have to be where I have to be.'

'Yes, me too.'

They walked without talking out of Covent Garden to Soho and the Bar Italia. Frith Street was a quiet spot away from the festivities, and the place was almost deserted. A TV high on the wall flickered its satellite message, deepening the colourless dusk. In window seats at the front of the narrow room, two old men sat side by side, blank faces pitted like decaying fruit. Dean asked for a mocha and stepped aside to allow Alberto, after a moment's hesitation, to order a white Americano. The Italian suggested they sit where they could talk more freely, so they went outside and huddled in their coats on the pavement, where a brisk wind carried hints of chocolate and whisky.

'In Manhattan,' Alberto observed in the measured tones of a cautious academic, 'there are thousands of cafés like this one, but with more character, more….' He cast around for the word but failed to find it. 'I wonder, have you ever been to New York?'

'Have I ever left London? Sometimes it seems not.' It was a myth, he realised then, that he passed the four seasons within city limits, the ring-roads of the metropolis, entirely voluntarily. There'd been so many attempts to leave, in fact, but each time he was drawn back by a twitch on the thread. 'I never go anywhere, actually – but I have been a mental traveller. *I've heard and seen such dreadful things as cold earth-wanderers never know.'*

Alberto glanced at him suspiciously. 'You know sometimes I find it hard to follow you, Dean.'

He shrugged and laughed. After all, why should they be able to communicate? What was this strange universal that included both of them? 'So where is it you have to be tonight?'

'I have a date with Carrie. You remember Carrie, right? She says she knows you'

'Carrie? Oh, yes, Carrie,' he laughed, 'I see. So *that's* what you decided to do.'

'How about you?' Alberto looked away down the twilit street; he seemed detached, even bored, and Dean tried not to ask himself what they were doing together. An attempt to tie up loose ends, it could be – but what end wasn't loose? This little chat could last for half a second or for the rest of their lives. But he sneaked his hipflask from his pocket and took a hit, and his mind went quiet again.

'There's a party tonight down in Camberwell. Have you ever been to Camberwell? You should see it sometime – it's the gateway to the south.' When Alberto looked over at him mirthlessly, Dean tried a different tack. 'So how's it going with old Carrie? Spill the beans, daddio.'

'I suppose you'll tell Laura anything I tell you.'

'You mean Laura is kept in the dark about your antics? Really, what way is that to behave? This is the end of the 20th century – you should be bringing your girlfriend home to dinner, getting your wife and mistress to pick out clothes for you together. We're on the cusp of a new millennium. They could even be friends!'

Alberto, failing to see the joke, threw up his hands in mock amazement. 'Dean, Dean, Dean, we don't all regulate our lives nil percent, as you do. Why would I want my girlfriend to hang out with my wife? Do I look like a sadist?'

A waitress appeared before them, an Italian girl with black bangs and brown eyes filled with a kindly light. She asked them whether they wanted anything else, dropped a couple of amaretti on their table, and wished them happy Christmas. Her heart-shaped face would once have filled him with excitement, but tonight he saw a change in himself, as if her good looks were a measure of his fall from grace. Such a woman was beyond him now, with the life he'd chosen; he could never make her understand his priorities or the reasons for his laughter, and she would only baffle him with the simplicity of her needs.

He glanced across the table at the Italian, whose eyes also followed the waitress. 'It's not a question of sadism, Alberto. Why cling to your uptight old-world mindset? Laura would respect you more if you told her what was going on.'

'Really, Dean, you are so full of shit.'

Dean leaned back and opened the biscuit with his teeth. 'As a matter of fact, Laura and I haven't seen each other for a while.'

'You've had a tiff.'

'We're taking a break.'

Alberto's phone buzzed in his pocket, but he ignored the buzzing, took off his hat and laid it on the table between their empty mugs. 'I suppose you think you gave her what she needed.'

'Maybe I did,' he shrugged, popping the little biscuit in his mouth. 'If a pigeon died in Assisi, would you blame Saint Francis?' His companion stared at him for an instant, then shook his head and looked away. The night was growing colder; the wind had dropped, but in its place had come the clammy graveyard feel so typical of the city at that time of year. 'Tell me, Alberto. What do you really think of your wife?'

'I think she's cracked, actually. She picks men up and flings them away like a used dishcloth.'

'She finds the flaws in us, it's true.'

'You probably won't believe this, Dean, but I was once a ladies' man of sorts.'

'Why shouldn't I believe it? We all have our hour in the sun.'

'Five years ago they even thought of me as a charmer. Now when I go to a party they walk around three walls to avoid me. But it was Laura who broke my spirit.' Alberto paused to exhale. 'She seemed so sweet and affectionate at first – well, you know how she snows you.'

'She's still very nice about you behind your back.'

'Don't lie to me, Dean.' Their waitress looked over from the doorway as Alberto raised his voice; even the two old fixtures shifted slightly in their seats, a stirring in the dust of ages. 'As soon as we got married she went on the attack, told me I was a pedant and a social leper, I was this and I was that.'

'Thissa and thatta,' laughed Dean. 'Oh sing me no more songs of sad Clapham.'

'Did you ever find out what makes her tick? Honestly, I would be glad to know – and that is some concession, Russler.'

He felt for the reassuring rectangle of the flask in his pocket. The dusk had been replaced in a stroke by darkness – theatrically, in this theatre district – flashing with the lights of angry drivers.

'Laura is Emma Bovary in a Liberty dress.' He lit another cigarette and was surprised to see the smoke hang in the air before his face, caught in the downward shaft from the streetlamp, as if time had momentarily frozen. 'Monogamy wouldn't suit her – she was born to spread herself thin. And you know, Alberto, it's not her fault that you chose the wrong woman.'

'She should have told me what she was like before we got married.'

'She expected you to have some intuition.' The Italian's petulance was vaguely irritating, like the engine left running a hundred metres up the street while the driver poked his head into a tattoo parlour, the car going nowhere but its noise filling every last pocket of the dull air. 'She thought you'd be an intellectual escort who filled her with his seed now and then, not some brainy leech who clung to her whenever she left the room.'

Alberto stubbed out his cigarette. 'There really is no gate on your mouth, is there Dean?'

'Allow me to make a suggestion.'

'Please don't.'

'Rise above, Alberto. Stop looking for the truth in every throwaway remark – and when you get home at night watch some bad TV, drink beer instead of wine. Loosen up, yeah,' he went on dreamily, his mind drifting from the subject and away from Frith Street, once his street of dreams – because, when he thought about it, he remembered everything – and along to Dean Street. 'Yeah, lighten up Alberto.'

Springing to his feet, the Italian slammed a handful of change on the table and stalked off. A moment passed while he watched him plod away down the road to the corner with Old Compton Street; but then he rose and followed with the abandoned fedora. He caught up with Alberto on Charing Cross Road and handed him his hat – and there they stood toe to toe in a blizzard of singletons out on blind dates, married saps and sad divorcees, all with faces like thunder. He felt a sudden shock of isolation in this storm of people, as if he'd just checked in with the world after some time out of it and found it even dingier than he recalled. In that moment, anything but solitude was acceptable, and he steered them to The Cambridge, where like a

213

miracle they found a table in the melee. The crush was appalling as he went to the bar to get their drinks, and he would have given up on the whole thing and walked on out the door – but there was, in fact, no party in Camberwell that night, and he needed to talk to someone at least remotely connected to him, someone he vaguely knew.

'I'm sorry, Alberto,' he said, coming back with a round of watery lagers and chasers of Jim Beams. 'I've behaved abominably, I know I have.'

Alberto only lifted his pint and drank; he seemed to have forgotten about his date with Carrie. They sat in the centre of it all, hemmed in by the London business classes; up at the bar in their suits, stocky geezers and skinny broads rocked with laughter at everything and nothing, waving £50 notes in the barmaids' faces. The men were easier to dismiss, of course, as they hid behind each other in their packs, blending into one man with a fat wallet; but the women hanging solo with hands on hips traced an outline of male inadequacy, as if illustrating the hollowness of all their aspirations.

'Just look at those people,' Alberto said. 'They think Mantovani wrote operas and Dante drove a bus – they're ignorant and *proud* of it.'

In an act of penance, Dean fought his way to the bar and bought another round. He didn't feel truly repentant – how could he – but he felt a flush of fellow feeling for someone as crushed as he was by this army of galoots. So they drank side by side on their stools but somewhat askew, two people naturally averted from each other, making clumsy attempts at candour. It was hard to be at ease with a man when you'd despoiled his home and danced a victory dance between his sheets. But the alcohol worked its magic; after another round, this time bought by Alberto, Dean's mood ascended the arc of his intake, and even the soldiers for stupidity seemed innocent. For a minute or two, he felt again the beautiful confusion that was the only real point of getting drunk – but Alberto's downcast face brought home to him the facts of life, their shared failure, that useless mix of envy and contempt, their slave standing in this great economy. What had he been doing while all these people were building their empires?

He was drunk now, in the state he was born to, but still it always took him by surprise whenever he reached it. His fingers slithered in the condensation on his glass as he stared at the floor between his feet, feeling that something was missing, something that was normally there. Whatever it was, he must have left it somewhere – but not only could he not recall what he'd left behind, all at once he couldn't say where it was he'd been or when, or any of the things he'd done in any of the places he couldn't remember.

'You know what I would have liked to be?' Alberto was talking to him, leaning across the table, breaking in on his thoughts. Some time must have passed between them in silence. The hour felt oddly late, as if they'd skipped ahead to the next stage, to that always messy phase between dinner and midnight when things would begin to unravel, resolutions would be unmade, promises broken, a phenomenon that in his life he'd loved and hated, resented and feared, because none of it was ever under his control. At any rate, whatever they'd planned to do that night had already happened without them. 'I would've liked to have been a courier in the ancient world,' Alberto was saying, 'on foot you know, on the one good road, carrying messages from Alexandria to Constantinople.'

Dean felt it turn on in him, the rare access to words that came and went in these states, whenever he mixed whisky with beer or wine with rum. 'The problem with guys like us,' he began – and then he stopped, unsure what the problem was but certain there was one. In a minute they swung by again, the words, like old friends dropping in on his mouth. 'The problem is we're too past it to be slackers and too bourgeois to be beatniks.' He tried to focus on Alberto, but for one mad instant couldn't find him in the room at all, although the guy was definitely sitting across from him. But there he was again suddenly, gazing back like some unfocused mirror image. 'We're like couriers in the modern world, taking some crappy envelope from Tobacco Dock to John Ruskin Street.' As he spoke, the room vanished altogether, and he had a vision as clear as a memory of falling on the road from Marathon, felled by Oedipus and rolling in the ditch – where he remained for so long, for the rest of ancient history, unseen by those who rode past in their chariots, invisible even to gods and goddesses.

The Italian gazed at him, his eyes swimming, floating nearer and farther as if they were both submerged, lost in a barroom in Atlantis. 'Did you ever have an ambition, Dean?'

'I wanted to be a poet once.'

Alberto continued to gaze at him with glassy eyes, afloat. 'And do you still write poetry?'

'No, yes. Only with my feet.' He was about to laugh in the face of his companion's blank look – but then, all at once, he needed him to grasp his meaning, with the urgency of someone who's just discovered his own truth. 'I'm a flâneur,' he said, 'I walk from page to page and write in footsteps, but no one sees me and nobody knows.'

The words as soon as they left his mouth were swallowed up in the incredible Christmas racket – he couldn't hear himself speak and didn't know exactly what he was saying. The other man's face swam up close, filled with malign knowledge, not of what he'd tried to show him but of something threatening and hard to resist.

'Because you are not a man without education, Dean, you will know that a *romance* was once just a story, one written in French. But then the meaning changed.' Alberto leaned back in his seat, clearly delighted to uncover the key to the text, and Dean was sucked forward in the wake of his utterance. 'It came to mean a story with scenes that had little to do with real life.' Alberto leaned towards him again, spitting now for emphasis. '*Little to do with real life*. Does that sound at all familiar to you, Dean?'

Dean leapt up and his stool crashed behind him, but Alberto came after and caught him by the arm at an exit blocked by a bouncer, a giant in his way. The bouncer made no attempt to intervene; he must have thought they were just talking the way men talk in pubs; he glared as if oblivious to them at the wall above their heads while the Italian pinned him with the ease of relative sobriety against a fruit machine, its blips and peeps punctuating his every sentence. Alberto had grown taller, or so it seemed, and he thrust his face in close to Dean's, whispering or yelling – it was hard to tell in the churn of voices above the fruit machine's absurd commentary.

'Do you know what Laura always said about you, Dean?'

'What? No.' He held up his hands to fend off the declaration to come, but his thumbs seemed tangled together.

'She would talk to me about you when we went to bed, complain. At the time of course I found it distasteful, but then I could only see that you had the upper hand, I believed you were winning, even when she told me you were a source of frustration.' The Italian pronounced his snippets of vernacular, *source of frustration*, *upper hand*, with a parodic sneer, as if laughing at the language itself. 'She called you Peter Pan, the Lost Cause, the Last Romantic.'

'Did she now? That's so sweet.' Dean struggled against the machine, trying to catch the bouncer's attention – but there was no escape.

'She would *rail* against you, Dean. How did she put it exactly? *He never knows who to run with, the fox or the hounds.* Do you get what she means, Dean? I know, but only because I asked – because I hardly ever get what she says, because she doesn't care if I understand. But that time she explained.' He thrust his hand in Dean's face, as if some final word was written on his palm. 'She said you could have chosen to be someone, but you chose to be nobody. You are *nobody*, Dean.'

Energised by the awfulness of this obituary, he flailed away from the Italian's grasp and broke free at last, pushing past the bouncer and heading for the Underground. He sensed Alberto close behind, on his tail – he must have read his mind. If it was the last thing he did, he had to talk to Laura, who knew who he was and still loved him, the only one.

# The Wrong Train

By the time the two men stood together on the southbound platform of the Northern Line, in the foul air warmed by its passage through miles of obscurity, Dean had forgotten why he'd gone down there. Standing in those grimy gusts, swaying on his feet behind the yellow line, he felt the Italian's advantage over him as sudden and final – and he saw his emaciated corpse on the desert floor, dogs feeding on his carcass, no spirit rising. The vision lasted only a moment, but an essential moment in which he ceased to believe in his life's grand sweep, its swift and thoughtless course through tunnels and over bridges, where flashes of sunlight answered long and echoing runs through the dark. Until now, he'd never doubted that his way of life was sacrosanct; but now he was full of doubt.

Looking back down the flickering path from his twenties into his thirties, he saw himself as others must have seen him, opened his ears to their voices, heard them ask why he hadn't done as they'd done, and why he hadn't done anything else. He could have been a monk, at least, living on a mountainside and praying for the world while the world went on with its work. But instead he'd set out on a bright day at the start of spring, wandered through the forest to a clearing, placed himself in a pleasant patch between trees and waited for everyone to join him. Of course, they never had joined him – why would they, when they all had things to do? So he'd gone from one leafy glade to the next, always expecting them to come and play even when it was obvious they weren't coming, and meanwhile combing his hair just right or fiddling with a buckle on his shoe, altering some small thing about what he did, moving an inch to the left to see better the setting sun or rising moon. It was true, yes, it was true that sometimes he drew a picture of the setting sun or rising moon and showed it to a tree, but that was all he did. It seemed amazing to him now that he never once thought of leaving his forest and going to look for the rest of the world. And in the meantime he'd memorised the pattern on every leaf, read the runes as written in sticks and twigs, made believe the birds just sang for him – all nothing, and all seen by no one but the all-seeing eye of the Other. Yes, he'd screwed around in the eyes of the Other while the Other looked on in contempt. He'd wasted his time.

But now the journey was over. He watched evening commuters and filthy sides of trains flash past, feeling rooted to the spot, as if he were the only person in the world who'd stopped moving. He might have turned on his heel and retraced his steps, gone back to the bar – or he might have stumbled to Lincoln's Inn Fields and passed out under a bush. But for some reason he stayed where he was, on the southbound platform of the Northern Line; and for some reason, although there were no forks in the line and any train might have taken him to Clapham, Alberto stood at his side, as if waiting for something else not a train, something he'd always wanted to see. Every few minutes a train went by with a whoosh – but it seemed there was a right train and a wrong train, and all these trains were wrong, and the two men stayed where they were in the grubby yellow light.

Dean swayed, dizzy with doubts, until he remembered what he'd set out to do, to call Laura, talk to someone who loved him. He searched his pockets but couldn't find his phone – and then it came to him that he had no pockets, wasn't even wearing his coat. He must have left it behind, the one he bought just the other day. He'd even lost his hipflask; his satchel was nowhere to be seen. Thinking back to the last time he saw it, he couldn't begin to name the hour when they'd become separated. In the milling crowd, he began to divest himself of his remaining possessions. He flung down his brown suede jacket, ripped at his old silk shirt until the buttons wheeled away, pulled over his head the stained t-shirt with its little dope holes that he used as a vest. He was kicking off his Docs when Alberto gripped him roughly by the arm. But Dean shook him off, scraped off his socks and stood in his bare feet on the chilly filth of the southbound platform, where people mumbled and jumbled and paid him no heed.

Another wrong train pulled in, and people climbed aboard. The doors began to close and were wrestled apart by a man in a raincoat; when the guard barked a warning over the PA, the man fell forwards into the carriage. Time started up again and ran as it had always run, with no pauses for reflection, and Dean saw how close he stood to the edge. He stepped back, keeping his eyes on a girl who winked at him as the train moved away, her tongue flicking across her lips. And then she was gone, as the train drew cool air in its wake, vanishing forever into the dark tunnel dotted with red lights and trailing rusty wires. He shuddered to think of that endless warren, caked with the cadavers of rats and mice, a million undiscovered dirty things.

He forgot his near nakedness and turned to go, leave the station perhaps or go to the northbound line and go home – but he must have turned one too many times, and he found himself again facing the edge. And his feet kept walking, although Alberto sprang up before him, wavering like an apparition, stretched to a long black thinness like a shoelace or a priest in a hall of mirrors. Alberto's hand grabbed at his elbow, but a moment too late to catch him, and he flew through time and space and the warm grey air. It did feel like flying, actually, but he no longer trusted his senses – so he did what he'd always done, he went with the flow. But the falling sensation brought his stomach to his throat, and his vomit flew ahead of him, hanging in the air as it left his mouth, a stream of ugliness that had been his brunch, a brown river thick with twisting snakes.

'Look at that,' he said out loud, 'I'm really dying!'

The thought made him laugh as he fell, and falling and laughing he watched his life stream out across the tracks – but it was a long fall, or so it felt, and then a bumpy landing. He banged his temple on a rail and broke his arm, or at least it hung uselessly at his side as he struggled for a foothold on surfaces slippery with rodent droppings. He put his good hand on the platform just as a rattle and hum announced the impending arrival of a train. He held it out, but no one came forward to help; the crowd seemed to stand and wave, some with tears in their eyes, as if saying salut, arrivederci, farewell. From behind the yellow line, they looked down at the man on the rails, intrigued by his plight – and from the perspective of his own dark realm, full of shit and dust and electricity, he saw the fascination in their eyes. There he was in the spotlight at last, a hero with a thousand faeces – but how had he fallen, why wasn't he wearing a shirt, and why was he laughing when he was injured and in danger? These were the questions of the hour; he saw them in the eyes of the crowd. Given time, they might have set them aside and found a way to hand him up – but there were no delays on the Northern Line that night, and time ran out for the curious crowd and the laughing man alike.

For Dean was laughing to the end. Shirtless and coated in flecks of vomit, his eyes crossed in an effort to see a way to safety, he laughed while the rails sang their song and the train shot towards him. Flinging his arms in the air in the moment before it arrived, he shouted a word that nobody heard – and then it caught him in his side, and he died instantly.

# Diary of a Ghost

Laura had always had a key to Dean's flat. She'd had it for almost as long as she'd known him, although she'd never used it in his lifetime. He'd handed it over one Sunday when they were walking on the Common, given it to her without comment, except to say it was his spare. At the time she'd simply pocketed it, thinking only that Dean, who had his foibles, had formed some expectation of her from a novel he'd read. Perhaps he'd made up a story in his head about a man of slender means with a rich mistress who discovers him at death's door and nurses him back to health. That was where he really lived, she sometimes thought, in the black and white melodramas of early cinema, when stardust was sprinkled over plotlines. In any case, early on she'd dismissed the idea of dropping in on him and discovering him in flagrante, but she'd never lost the key.

A few days into the new year, she left her husband to unshelve his books and finish his packing – he was not yet gone, but he was going – and took the Northern Line up to Camden to visit Dean for the first time. She opened the door to his flat and was struck by a blast of cold air; walking through, she found a window open in the bathroom and a pigeon in the bath – it left as soon as it saw her, in a feathery flurry. Her walk around the dead man's territory was initially fascinating; he was, after all, the first dead man she'd ever known. But after a few minutes, the absolute stillness between the piles of paperbacks, mounds of unwashed shirts and stacks of vinyl began to spook her. All these objects might have been loved in their day, but their lover's disappearance had left them looking as they must have looked on hooks and racks in charity shops, forlorn and bedraggled.

The drab apartment felt as unoccupied as if Dean had abandoned it many moons and not a few days ago, adding to its emptiness. The flat had a weird vacancy that distracted her from whatever she was looking for and made her think irrelevantly of its previous tenants, all those who lived there before him, where they might have gone and if they too had come to grief in some drunken accident. It didn't help that in the weeks before he died she'd had no contact with him; they hadn't even spoken on the phone. His death as reported in a few lines in the *Standard* and described in a shaky half hour by Alberto had made little impression on her – Dean was just a shade more absent, was all. But as she wandered through his rooms, she was gradually impressed by the fact of his extraordinary departure not just from her life but from the whole picture. She wanted to ask him what it was like, now that he'd finally left London, a thing she'd never known him to do.

In the lounge, she paused for a while by the mantelpiece above an unused fireplace, blocked with a piece of plywood painted over white. The mantelpiece was thick with dust, and under the dust was a collection of orange and green Rizla packets, a dual-language edition of *Les Fleurs du Mal*, a cassette tape that had come unspooled, and a little plastic Buddha. A photograph propped up at the end showed a young Dean Russler on a wide lawn with a river behind him and his arm around a girl. He looked not much more than 19. His gaze was so open and guileless that she wouldn't have known it was him if the picture hadn't been in his living room.

She glanced into the foul little kitchen with its view of air-con vents and crumbling chimney stacks, before moving on to his bedroom, where she sat down on his bed. How uncomfortable it was though, the mattress! How could he ever get to sleep on such a thing? She giggled furtively at the notion that perhaps all those times when he came round to sleep at hers, he just wanted somewhere nice to lie down. It really wasn't funny, she told herself – but actually it kind of was, or at least it was the kind of thing they would have found funny together. But it was obvious now why he'd never invited her over: he thought of her as someone who couldn't share a room as such awful curtains, such horrible tattered wallpaper, that hideous thin-weave carpet. The only scene for which these ugly props would have made sense was his death scene, when he lay on his deathbed and she wept into his stained shirt. And he was wrong and he was right, of course, because his room was revolting and she felt a bit sick – but how could he have been so stupid as to believe that her feelings for him could have been influenced by the state of his furniture?

Now that he was no longer there to have feelings for, her feelings turned to herself. Sitting on a dead man's bed gave her a strong sense of her own ghostliness – even bouncing a little and hearing the creak of its springs couldn't return her to her proper place in the world. The woman on the bed seemed light and airy and oddly ineffectual; she'd crossed the world a couple of times and left her mark on a heart or two, but those hearts would wither away in an empty chest and everything they'd felt would be forgotten.

Still she sat and bounced for a while, as the sunlight panned around and shone with cutting brightness through the westernmost window. Eventually she got up to fling it open, but the sash was broken and it moved less than an inch. The slice of air that came in was like ice, as she might have expected at the end of a winter afternoon – but she had a sudden craving for something from outside this barren space, domain of the single dead man. Sounds of cars poured in from Camden Road; the room was echoey with north London loneliness.

'It's so strange being here without you,' she said out loud – and as soon as she spoke, she saw herself as Dean would have seen her, a thorny English rose not dressed for the season, sitting on his bed in a yellow cotton number with little brown alligators, smeared at the waistline with blood, still waiting for him to come and do something wicked to her. 'In fact it's downright bizarre. I'm not sure I like it that much.'

But she sat on, waiting, as the sun neared the skyline, its bluish light staining the battered fronts of the buildings opposite. Aspects of his room became known to her, as minute by minute her boundaries became the parameters of his flat, a bachelor's paradise or bachelor's hell, a rickety shell with few contents, hanging in the blue air over a busy route. 'That's not just *blue*,' she could hear him say, 'it's agate blue, no, it's blue jay blue.' Kinds of blue – that was the kind of thing he'd argue about, when sufficiently alert. He must have done what she was doing now so many times, watched sunlight slant across his walls at this hour of the day, just sitting. And how had it made him feel, she wondered – inspired or suicidal, hopeless or tranquil? His states of mind had often struck her as arbitrary, dependent on nothing outside himself; he was a man of intense and changing moods, but she was never sure how much he cared what went on around him. If the world had come to an end on his watch, would it even have clouded his sky?

In the blueing light she became aware all at once of his satchel, which sat beside her on the bed and bounced whenever she bounced. It must have been there since she entered the room, but its sudden appearance took her by surprise even so. Things had a way of making their presence felt, she supposed. Seeing the satchel on the bed was almost like seeing Dean himself; it was his most faithful companion, he was never without it – but here it was, without him. Somehow he'd managed to leave it behind on his final trip.

The clasp was undone. She lifted the top and found herself holding his diary, a green ring-bound book with *1999* written on its cover in large black figures. She'd seen it before, of course, but never held it in her hands. Often in those tortuous weeks towards the close of summer she'd thought of sneaking off and reading it in her bathroom while Dean lay asleep on her bed. He always slept like a log – he need never have known. Only the fear of what she might find had stopped her from doing so. Now, when there was less at stake, she was still afraid – or perhaps it was more shyness than trepidation. They'd kept things from each other for a reason, after all, and even in his absence that reason remained. But she shut her eyes and opened the notebook halfway, then opened her eyes and read.

The pages were filled with an ornate black squiggle, with few corrections. Skimming, she marvelled at the sheer multitude of words. He'd been faithful after all, in his own fashion; he'd left nothing out, no detail was neglected. There were words for dull mornings, brilliant noons and burning dusks, changes in the weather and casts of light, taillights reflected in wet roads and cloudy skies in wet rooftops. There were words for hazy summer days spent in drunken recollection of other hazy summer days. At a glance, the sheer scale of his inventory was forbidding, almost frightening. She put the notebook aside, paced the room for a few minutes, lit a cigarette, and then lit the seven candles in a hefty brass candlestick on a table by the bed – some impulse buy from Oxfam, she guessed, which must have done him for a bedside light. Out in the fading day, a blackbird perched on a wire as if frozen, neither singing nor preening itself, while sodium lamps came on below. This was what Dean would have seen.

She turned back to the beginning of the notebook and read through the whole year from its start, skipping every second sentence, looking for herself in the text. And there she was, in the spring, present and real and radiant for a moment – but then she went missing for pages on end, as if she'd never been. Dean had divided the year up under headings, giving each phase of experience a silly and pretentious subtitle, such as **Selfish Nature**, **Infernal Effervescence**, **Your Turn My Turn**, **The Trouble Bubble**. Despite appearing to drift through life quite aimlessly, he'd had a system of sorts; the recording angel couldn't work in conditions of complete disorder. She was there sometimes under some headings and totally absent under others: she cropped up in **Roses and Flavours** and was all over the section he called **Bourgeois Subterfuge**, but then nowhere at all in **A Date with Fate**, **Dark Avenues** or **Saving Grace**.

The headings were in any case no indication of the content, which was unvarying in its theme, astonishingly so. His universe hadn't been parallel but set apart, to one side, as if on a promise never to touch anyone else's world. It was made up almost entirely of momentary occurrences of no obvious import. She read on through Dean's account of the year, looking for anything familiar to her in his vast index of sky colours and wind directions, graffiti tags and broken kerbstones – the intense particulars of petals scattered across a grassy verge, a squirrel lying squashed beneath a tree, an unusual mark spotted on a pavement, a blind in a window that he passed every day that was sometimes open and sometimes closed. Whatever meaning these things had for him was left unsaid, although she searched through all the particulars for something stronger than a hint – a declaration of some kind, a statement of intent. It would have been unlike him to make such statements, she was aware; but she went on reading, driven by a need to know that for a while went on growing with every turn of the page.

As the pages went on, however, her need was steadily overcome by boredom. Of course, he wrote an elegant sentence now and then, and at first she admired his fidelity to every tiny fluctuation in ambience; but by the time she got into September, with its leaves and mists and mists and leaves, she was weary of his compulsive collecting of ordinary events. In his attention to these minutiae there was a flatness, a dryness; this urban Thoreau had sometimes been dull. She'd read enough of rains running into gutters and rising suns glinting from all the various things that a sun could glint from – she wanted to see people, people as they lived and breathed, feelings crossing faces.

One face, not hers, was described over and over, although it was a face that hardly ever seemed to change, a face that wore a frown that never turned upsidedown but only deepened – except at the moment of climax, of course, when 'all her features

235

ran into one.' The face had lips that never seemed to speak, but he made out their shape in line after line, drew in word after word the lines of that 'million dollar mouth.' It hung over everything for page after page, section after section; but even that silent face vanished from the record as autumn lengthened into winter, as if he could no longer bear to recall its strange attractions.

The final pages of the journal, under the heading **Dubious Epiphanies**, were littered with a litany of varying shades from steel grey to coal black, dark colours abstracted from form almost. Occasionally he came up with something more personal, lonely scribbles, as if he'd retired to the corner of a bar to scrawl his name in vain. And then the diary ran out, several days before his death – came to a full stop, with no conclusion, unless she was to read into his two last entries some deeper insight, one he'd not had before, which to him was startling and fresh.

> One thing I've learnt this year is that people should stick to their own tribe. So in future I'll be more realistic – find myself a secretary in a canary-yellow skirt and settle down with her in zone 6, give up all my vinyl and the rest of my crap and just worship her narrow hips. We'll work side by side in our open-plan office, typing letters dictated to us by the walking heart attack who is our boss, then we'll fuck all

night like two lovebirds. That was always me –
I just never saw it till now.

And then, at the turn of the page:

> I see them walk about with their hands in each
> other's pockets, incandescent with happiness,
> and realise I've never had a soulmate. But then
> I'm not sure I'd want one. There'd be no means
> of escape – no parting from her. Once mated,
> our souls would remain forever in each other's
> realm, having deeply unsatisfactory ghost sex
> until the end of time. So what should I do
> instead? Faute de mieux, I suppose I could kiss
> someone new, wake up in a stranger's bed again
> and skip out in the morning with my cock in a
> sling. It's worked for me before.

Night had come on while she'd been reading.
The discoloured rags acting as curtains hung in a
half-light cast by the candles and a sour orange that
came up from street level – so ugly, really, all that
blotchy light on blotchy walls. But ugliness, she
now knew, was close to his ideal of beauty.

'So this is what you were like,' she spoke into the
gathering darkness, 'when you were left to your
own devices.'

She closed the diary on its final entry and flung
herself back on the cold, hard bed with its busted
springs. In time a siren wailed, and she stood and

went to the bedroom window and watched an ambulance turn into Royal College Street. On the pavement below, a middle-aged woman with stringy hair and enormous spectacles dragged a linen sack full of her lumpy possessions away from Camden and further into the night. When she turned to face the room again, Dean stood before her, perplexed but complacent as was his way, not remotely worried that he might have disappointed her. It was exactly the look he would have given her if he'd found her reading his diary when he was alive. She smiled – it was good to see him again – and his spirit came closer until their faces almost touched.

'But your writing is so *beautiful*, Dean,' she murmured, and his face lit up. 'I mean your *handwriting*,' she added, laughing – and he gave one last grimace at her irony and dissolved into the chill air.

Laura blew out the candles, put on her coat and went out into the street. Back at the house, Alberto would be waiting for her with his boxes in the hallway, his endless packing like some Herculean task; when it was finished he, too, would disappear. She still carried the diary, had walked away with it, without thinking. She understood its author now, and knew what she'd been to him – at best a naked underling in his sensational life and at worst an intellectual freak, a walking joke book. In truth, she didn't feel much like laughing although, if it had happened to someone else, she might have found it funny. But no, it wasn't funny at all. At the corner by the Underworld, she stopped and held up the notebook with its jumble of yearnings and revulsions and the whole bland secret of their brief time together and gave it one last shake, hoping that something would fall from between its leaves, but nothing fell.

In her path was a black municipal bin with Camden on its side and LITTER in gold letters, and she thrust into it the diary and threw in after it the key to his flat. Then she crossed over to the station and sank to platform level on the escalator, taking in the little adverts for razors and soap on the wall and pale oval faces of people rising the way she'd come. She sank down way below ground level, unburdened of Dean and his world, lighter by one spectre. At home she would pour herself a glass of wine, run herself a bath and masturbate once in his memory maybe, to milk the last few drops of a feeling that had once been so full. And in the morning when she opened her eyes he would just be dead. It would be a new morning, she thought, stepping off the end of the moving stairs, not like all the old ones; there was nothing left of *them*. Those old mornings had had their day, she thought – and this time she did laugh. She would always have found that funny, the thought that old mornings could have had their day. She would have laughed at such a silly notion long before she met Dean or Alberto or all the other studs and fanny rats, when all men were just her dad, as a child growing up on the edge of the Salisbury Plain.

It was a day in midweek, a Wednesday perhaps, but days at the start of a year never seemed to come in any special order, and she wasn't entirely sure. There was a definite lull, in any case, a sense that all activity had ceased at least for the moment, almost everything had come to a halt and no business was being done – and the Underground, for once, was almost empty. Only one other person shared the platform with her, a man around her age who leaned against the wall, down at the far end, fiddling with his tie and reading a paperback. He glanced up in her direction and their eyes met, and in the same instant they smiled at each other and shook their heads. She stayed where she was, at her end of the platform, thinking about tomorrow – and the morning, fresh and unspoiled, when she'd get up to face the new reality.

# Afterword

*Anyone who catches my eye...* starts on the night of David Copeland's third bomb, the one he put in a bag in The Admiral Duncan on Old Compton Street on the last day of April 1999. The first two bombs he let off in Brixton and Brick Lane – he targeted in turn London's Afro-Caribbean, Asian and gay communities. Few people not targeted by that neo-Nazi bombing campaign remember these incidents; they not described as terrorism at the time and were overshadowed by the mystery of Jill Dando's shooting, which happened between the second and third bombs. It's fair to say that I probably wouldn't have taken them in myself, but I was back in London that spring after four years away and everything seemed very vivid – and I was quite close to the third bomb, though not as close as Dean.

Dean started life as a minor character in the first novel I ever tried to write, in the mid-1990s. In that novel he died too, accidentally blown up on a double decker bus somewhere near Greenwich by his ex-girlfriend's father, in a silly homage to Conrad's *Secret Agent*. The first version with Dean in a starring role was written in the summer of 1999 – a sunny and frivolous thing at that point, although it still ended with Dean's death. I typed it up and enlarged it in the summer of 2003, at which point it became a sort of touchstone in my life, even a refuge for my feelings, something I went back to whenever I needed a safe place to hide.

The 2003 version was still pretty short and shiny – by 2005, Dean's story had become so gloomy and distended that a reader at the Literary Consultancy described it as *irremediably bleak* – this when I still thought of it as my comic novel. Then I went back to it again in the summer of 2013, changing everything but the story itself, and again in the summers of 2017 and 2020.

Many things have been dropped from earlier versions: whole sections written from Alberto's POV, a long chapter in which Dean goes with Laura to visit her family in the west country, one where Dean takes a woman from work down to Brighton and another where he whisks Monika off to Cambridge for a rainy picnic. In earlier versions, when I was still wedded to mimicking the classical realism I'd admired as a teenager and still gave credence to some notion of bourgeois balance, there was even a *nice* couple called Simon and Rachel, friends of Dean's from university. The original story also had a longer coda, at the end of which Laura was allowed to fly off to Australia with a barman to start her new life. All these things were chopped out

– but still other things were added. It wasn't until 2013 that the novel began with the bomb, and it was only then that I allowed Monika and Laura to meet, an encounter that for all those years seemed so difficult to write that I didn't even really think about attempting it.

The title has also changed many times. It has gone from *Flicker*, which I had to scrap because it was used for a successful thriller, to *Weekend Lover* through *The King of Bohemia* to the title it had in 2005, *Anyone who catches my eye can have me*. In 2013 I thought it was a good idea to call it *The Flâneur*, which now seems a very grand name for this small and particular tale. For a few months it was called *White Plastic Cups*, an allusion to nineties shock art, a sort of Tracey Emin concept. But then it seemed too flimsy and cold for what is essentially a slightly distressed love story – so I went for a while with a line I remember seeing in my friend Sara's notebook in about 1992, *When I close my eyes I see almost everything*. But then David read it and said that of all these titles he preferred one of the ones I'd given it nearly twenty years ago, so *Anyone* it is.

It's true that Dean is a flâneur, more of an old-school Paris type than the sort of psychogeographer you might find in Iain Sinclair or Lee Rourke. The science of flâneurism never interested me much, but

I've done all the walks described in the novel at least once, redoing some of them with the narrative in mind, as well as the train and bus trips, such as the bus journey that takes Dean from Clapham to Streatham Hill. There are several points at which my life intersects with Dean's, but the only straight autobiography comes in the description of wandering around London in the autumn in the chapter *The Recluse*. That did happen – I was a flâneur myself, still am. The bars, pubs, cafés and restaurants are all ones I went to in my time, or in their time, because a lot of that has gone since 1999. But a lot of the effects of that environment are an invention of the novel, or transpositions from other texts. As well as mapping London as he goes through it, Dean is effectively creating his own city. The Soho he inhabits, or wants to inhabit, is in his head the Soho described in Daniel Farson's heartbreaking account of it in *The Gilded Gutter Life of Francis Bacon*. As far as I can see, the Soho of that era bears almost no relation to the Soho of 1999, but to Dean they are magically one and the same.

A great deal of the novel derives from other texts, of course, a fact that the text flags up on many occasions. For instance, the phrase *contingent and necessary* as a way to describe areas of London is taken from Iris Murdoch's first novel, *Under the Net*, a book that I read before I knew London very well and which has always influenced the way I see it. Although a lot of the Fitzgeraldian romance was taken out in the editing, *Gatsby* – with its violent episodes and loveless love story – is still a shaping presence, as are other novels of that length. Around the time when I first typed up the original story was when I first read *Giovanni's Room*, which on rereading I can see must have provided me with the closed-in feel of impending doom, as well as the pattern for a relationship founded on inequalities. *Vile Bodies* is another obvious starting point, particularly in the brittle satirical character of Laura.

But in the end, Dean's story isn't especially close to those narratives, which were so of their time but also aimed for a kind of permanence, a place in a history of such things, some kind of great tradition. In its raggedness and sense of place, *Anyone* more closely resembles – or at least I'd like to think so – the precious Brixton novels of Martin Millar, *Ruby and the Stoneage Diet* and *Lux the poet*, with their total disregard for the niceties of literary fiction, their happy one-offness and their heartfelt documenting of the margins.

# Acknowledgements

A project that has taken so much time to finesse has of course had many readers. The last two to touch this book were Håvar Ellingsen, who advised on formatting and assured me that it wasn't chockful of typos, and David Cromartie, who chose the final title from the long list given above. David was also the only person to read the miserable 2005 version of the novel, aside from Anna South for The Literary Consultancy, who I have to thank for her glorious demolition, much needed at the time. Susannah Waters ran a workshop somewhere in Sussex at the start of this century, where she read the first couple of chapters and made encouraging noises and good suggestions. She also facilitated the award of the TLC reading through Mark Hewitt at Lewes Live Literature. In that context I must also mention Elizabeth Ingrams, whose short story workshop for Spread the Word in 2006 had an alchemical effect on my writing.

The other decisive interventions on this novel were Russell Honeyman back in 2013, whose comments on Monika were especially salient, and James Swift in 2017, who got me back to this story after I'd let it lie and made helpful criticisms of both the start and the finish. But everyone who has read the novel over the decades has played a role in its development, some of which is visible in the text. In 2003, for example, Jonathan told me that there was 'too much sex and not enough furniture', a comment that greatly added to Laura's fetishistic attitude towards interior decoration. Russell's observation that the story had 'relentless pathos' seemed so apt that I found a place for the phrase in *Snow Leopards*. Imogen was the only person to read the whole thing twice without being asked, which was just so heartening. Richard's encouragement over the years has been incredibly important. In 2003, he said that Dean Russler was 'as iconic as James Bond'. It's a comparison that 007 might not be very keen on, but it fished me out of the depths at a particularly low moment.

Thanks to everyone not mentioned above who has read this story from its earliest stages, including mum, Kitty, Martie, Alva, Lena, Amina, Hugh, Kathy, Kerry, Katy, Ian, Saskia, the other David, Talulah, Giorgio from the long-gone Italian café on the corner of Stanley Road, Raquel, Brendan, Patrick, Liz, Gareth, Zoe, Julius, Mark, Eimear, Liam, Adrian, Penny, Martin and the other John. You have been the invisible collaborators.

– Sneinton, September 2021